ARF AND the THREE DOGS
by Philip Wooderson

ILLUSTRATED BY BRIDGET MACKEITH

COLORS BY JESSICA FUCHS

Librarian Reviewer
Laurie K. Holland
Media Specialist (National Board Certified), Edina, MN
MA in Elementary Education, Minnesota State University, Mankato, MN

Reading Consultant
Sherry Klehr
Elementary/Middle School Educator, Edina Public Schools, MN
MA in Education, University of Minnesota, MN

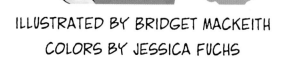

STONE ARCH BOOKS
Minneapolis   San Diego

First published in the United States in 2006
by Stone Arch Books,
151 Good Counsel Drive, P.O. Box 669,
Mankato, Minnesota 56002.
www.stonearchbooks.com

Originally published in Great Britain in 2003
by A & C Black Publishers Ltd,
38 Soho Square, London, W1D 3HB.

Library of Congress Cataloging-in-Publication Data
Wooderson, Philip.
    Arf and the Three Dogs / by Philip Wooderson; illustrated by Bridget
MacKeith.
    p. cm. — (Graphic Trax. Arf Mysteries)
    ISBN-13: 978-1-59889-021-1 (library binding)
    ISBN-10: 1-59889-021-2 (library binding)
    ISBN-13: 978-1-59889-177-5 (paperback)
    ISBN-10: 1-59889-177-4 (paperback)
    1. Graphic novels. I. MacKeith, Bridget. II. Title. III. Series.
PN6727.W66A76 2006
741.5—dc22   2005026689

Summary: Arf decides to use his mother's camera to make money as a reporter and
photographer. When he takes pictures of the neighborhood dogs, Arf realizes that
something strange is happening at the animal shelter.

1 2 3 4 5 6 11 10 09 08 07 06

Printed in the United States of America in Stevens Point, Wisconsin.
072009
005576R

TABLE OF CONTENTS

CAST OF CHARACTERS

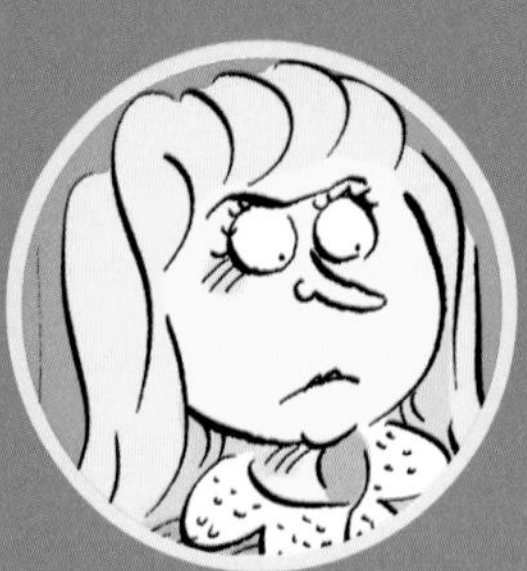

MOM

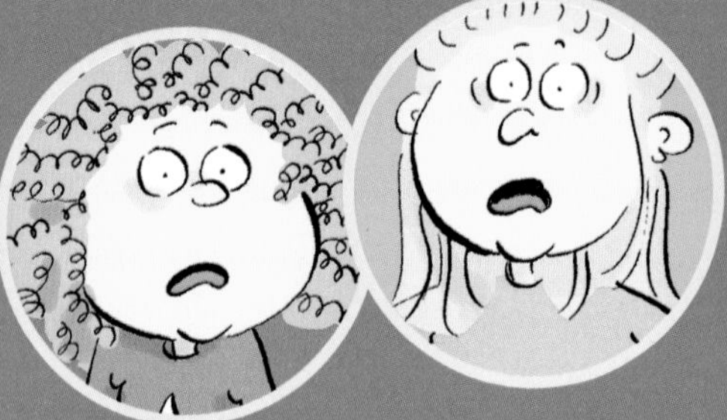

ARF'S SISTERS
(BEE & GLORIA)

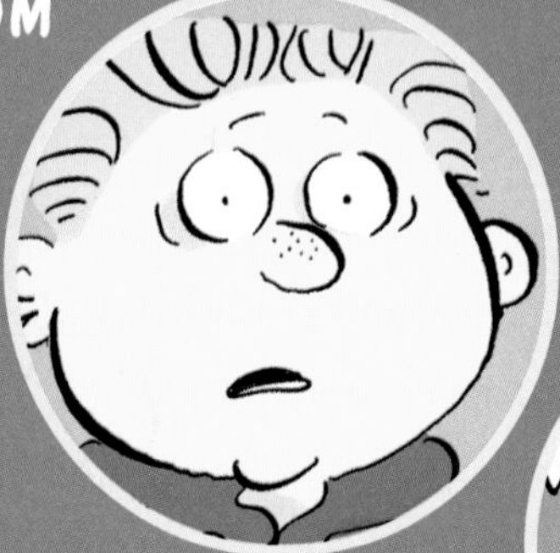

ARF

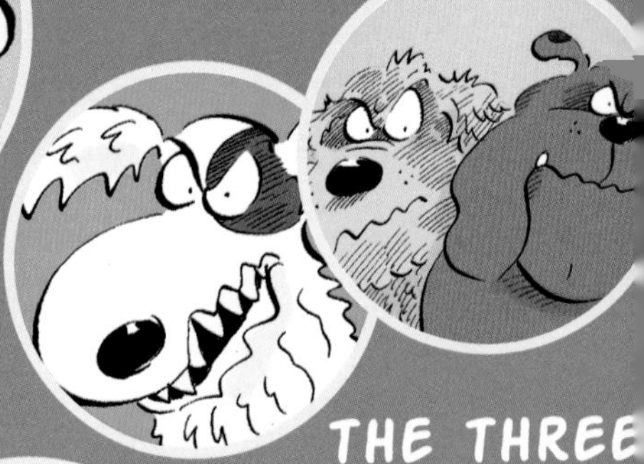

THE THREE
DOGS

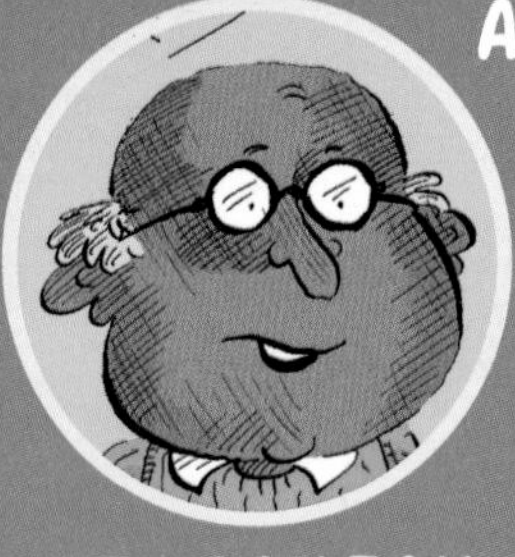

MR. SANJAY

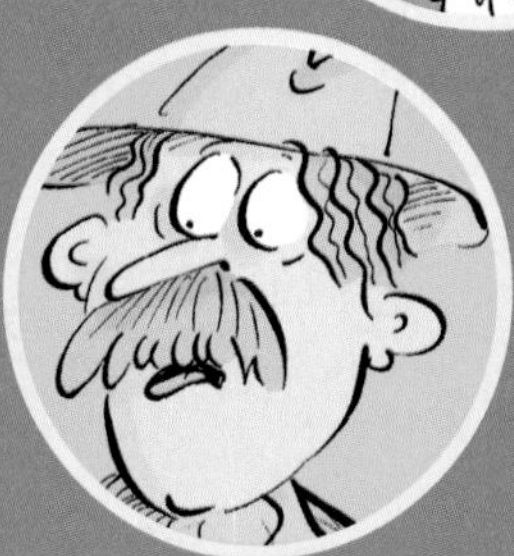

MAJOR NIMBY

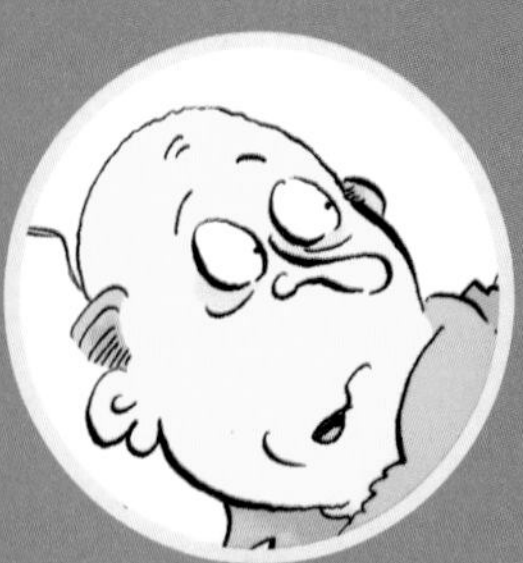

CRAZY BARNEY

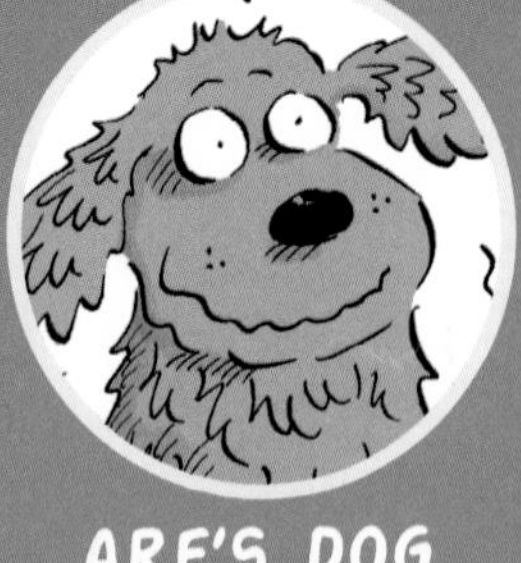

ARF'S DOG
(HOPPA)

CHAPTER ONE

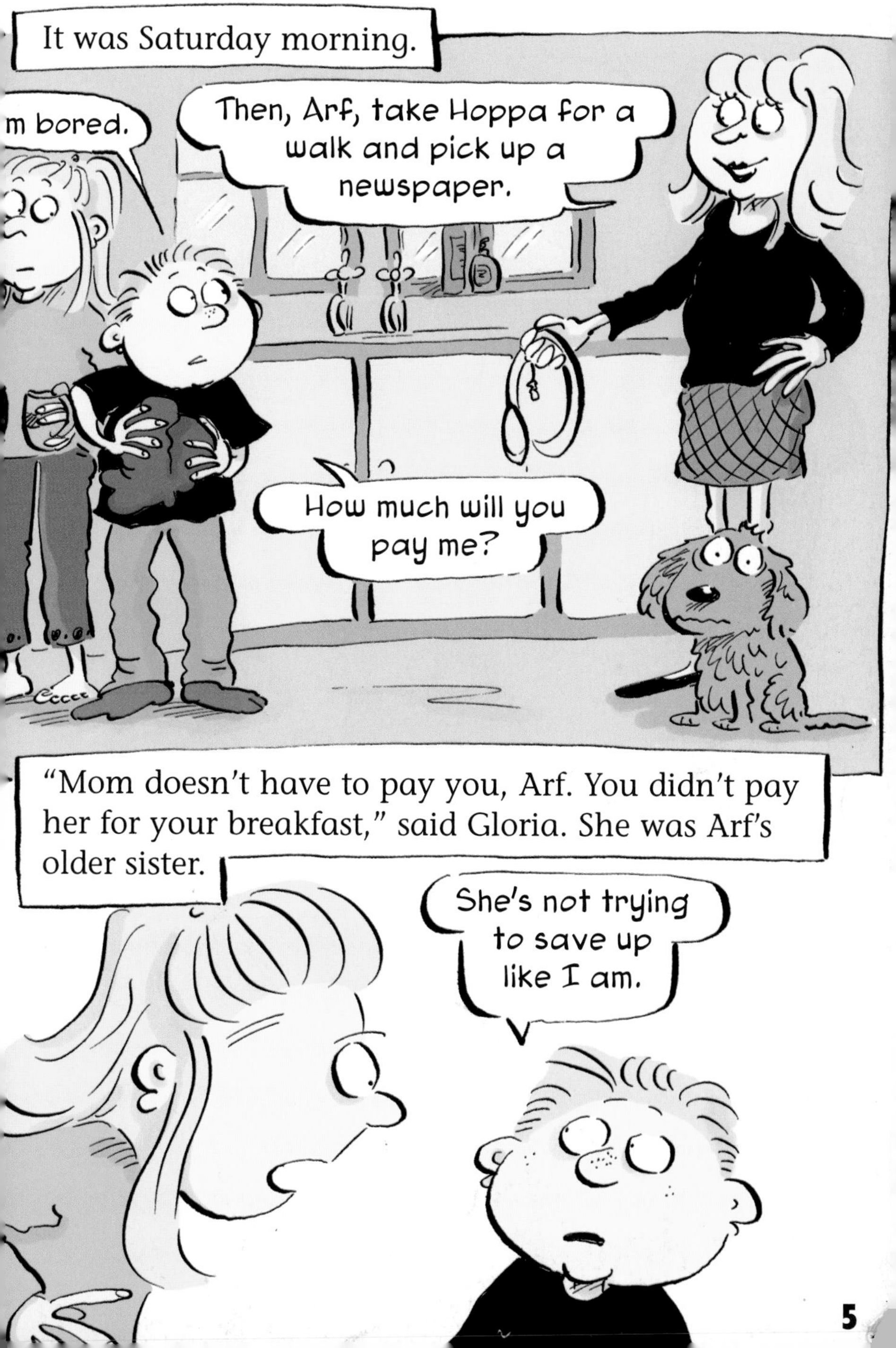
It was Saturday morning.
m bored.
Then, Arf, take Hoppa for a walk and pick up a newspaper.
How much will you pay me?
"Mom doesn't have to pay you, Arf. You didn't pay her for your breakfast," said Gloria. She was Arf's older sister.
She's not trying to save up like I am.

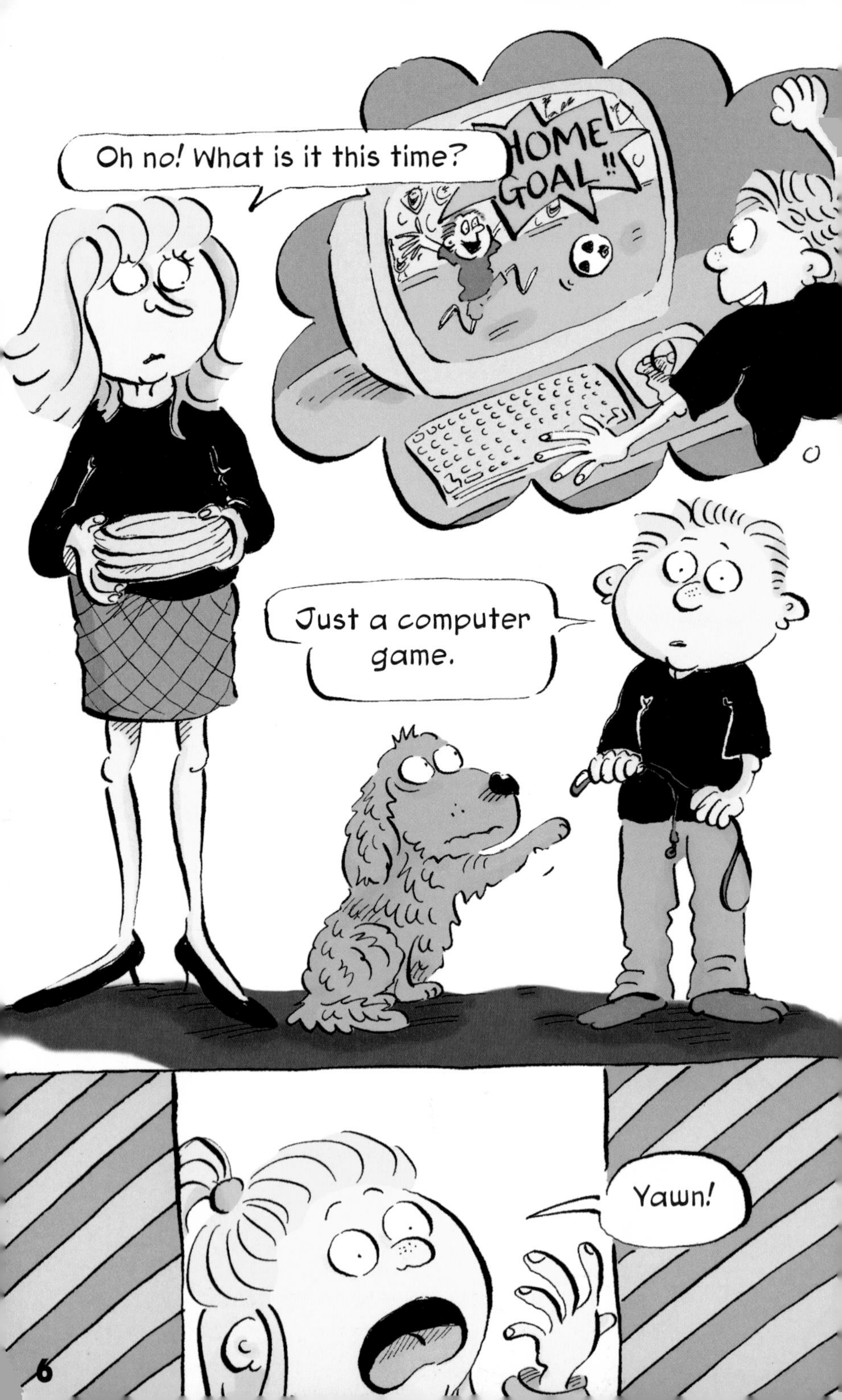
Oh no! What is it this time?
HOME GOAL!!
Just a computer game.
Yawn!

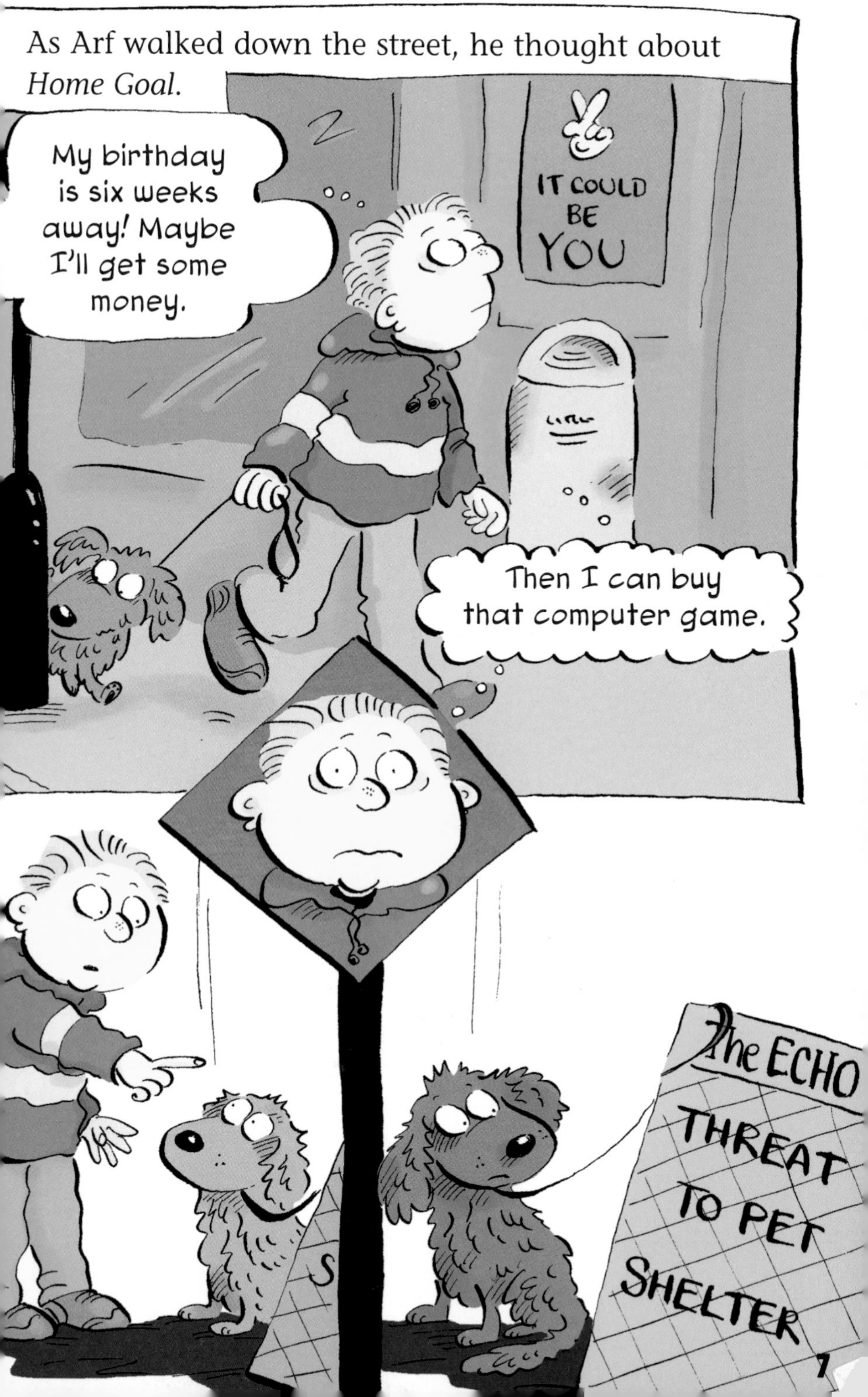
As Arf walked down the street, he thought about *Home Goal*.
My birthday is six weeks away! Maybe I'll get some money.
IT COULD BE YOU
Then I can buy that computer game.
The ECHO
THREAT TO PET SHELTER

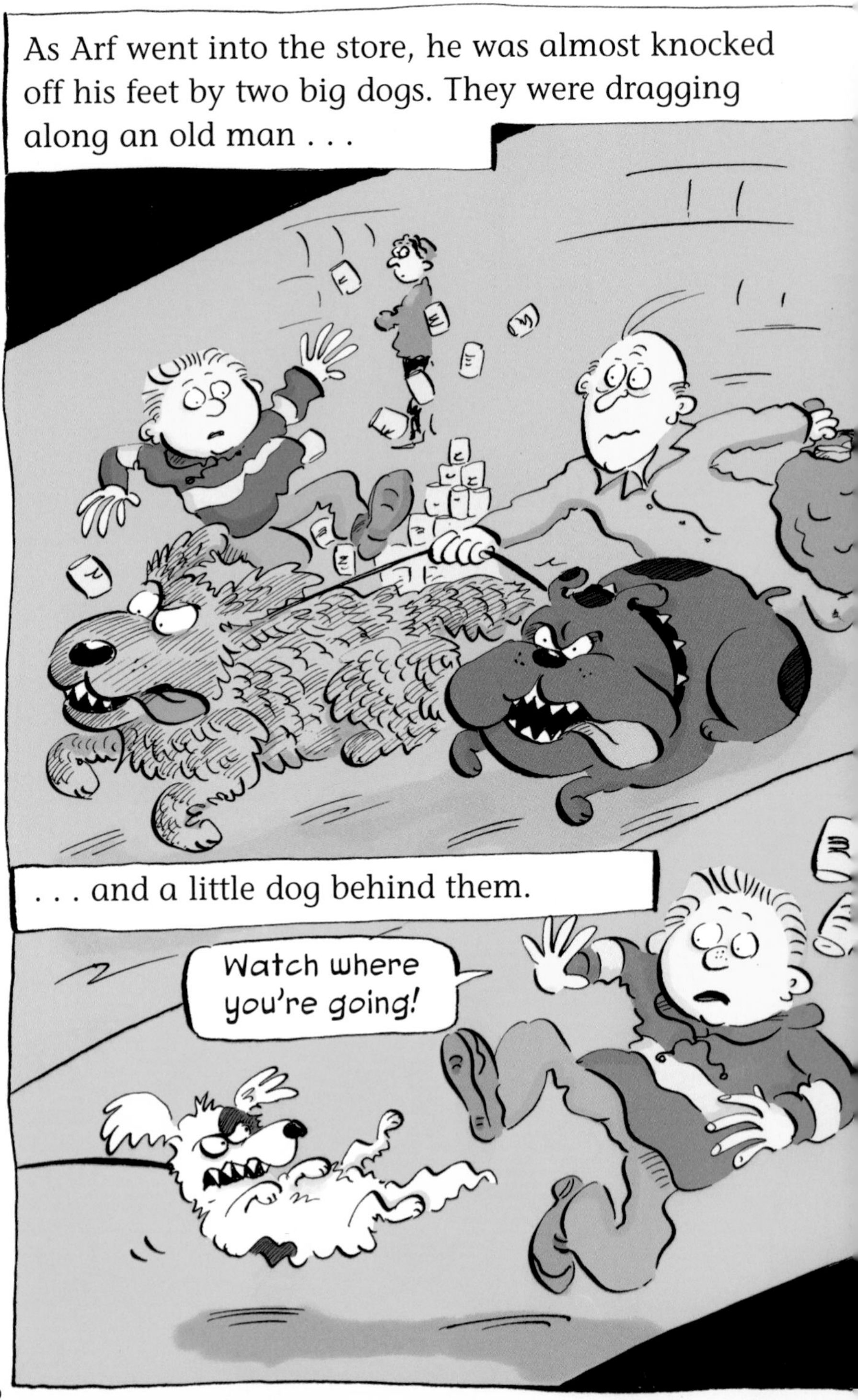
As Arf went into the store, he was almost knocked off his feet by two big dogs. They were dragging along an old man . . .
. . . and a little dog behind them.
Watch where you're going!

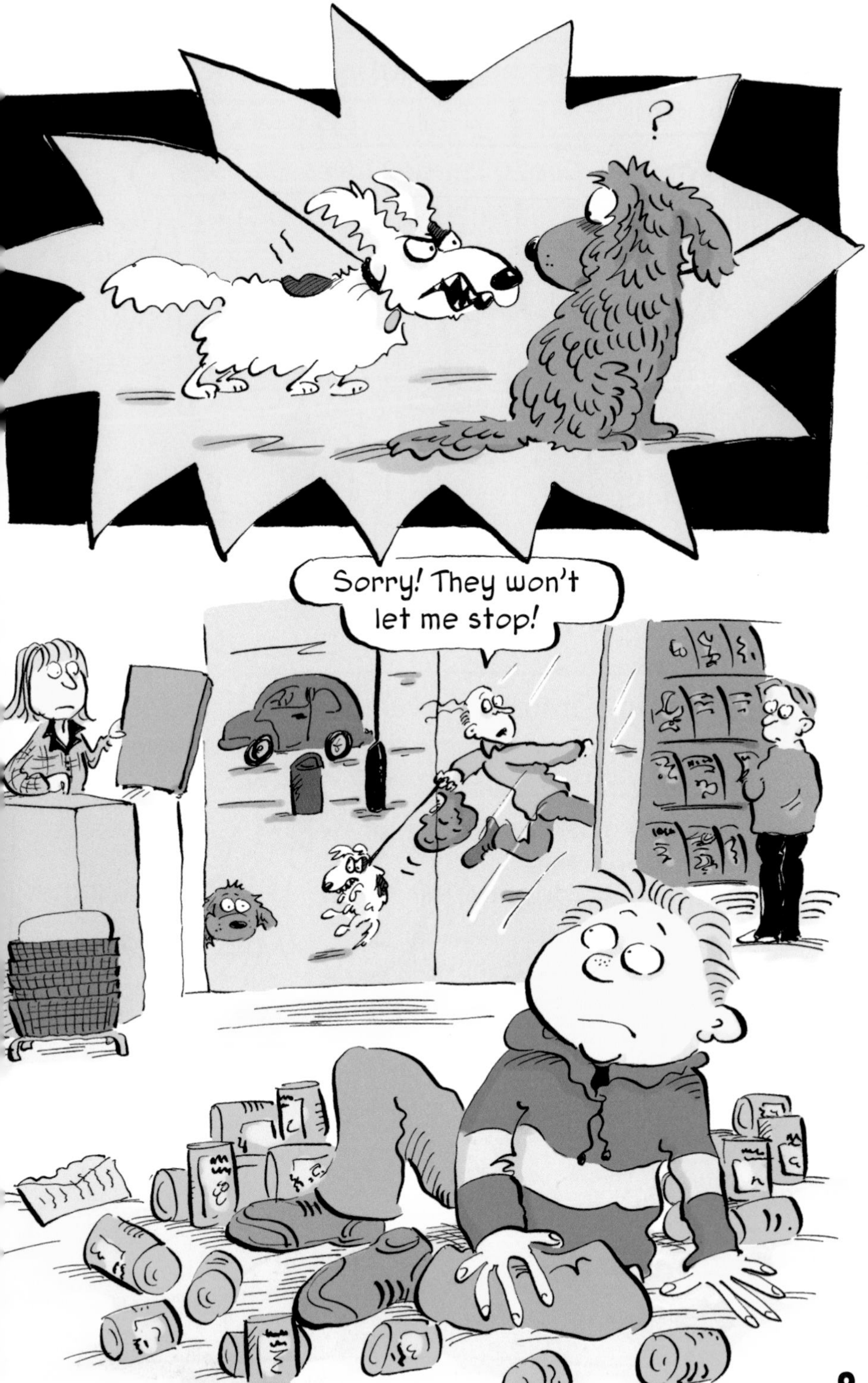
?
Sorry! They won't let me stop!

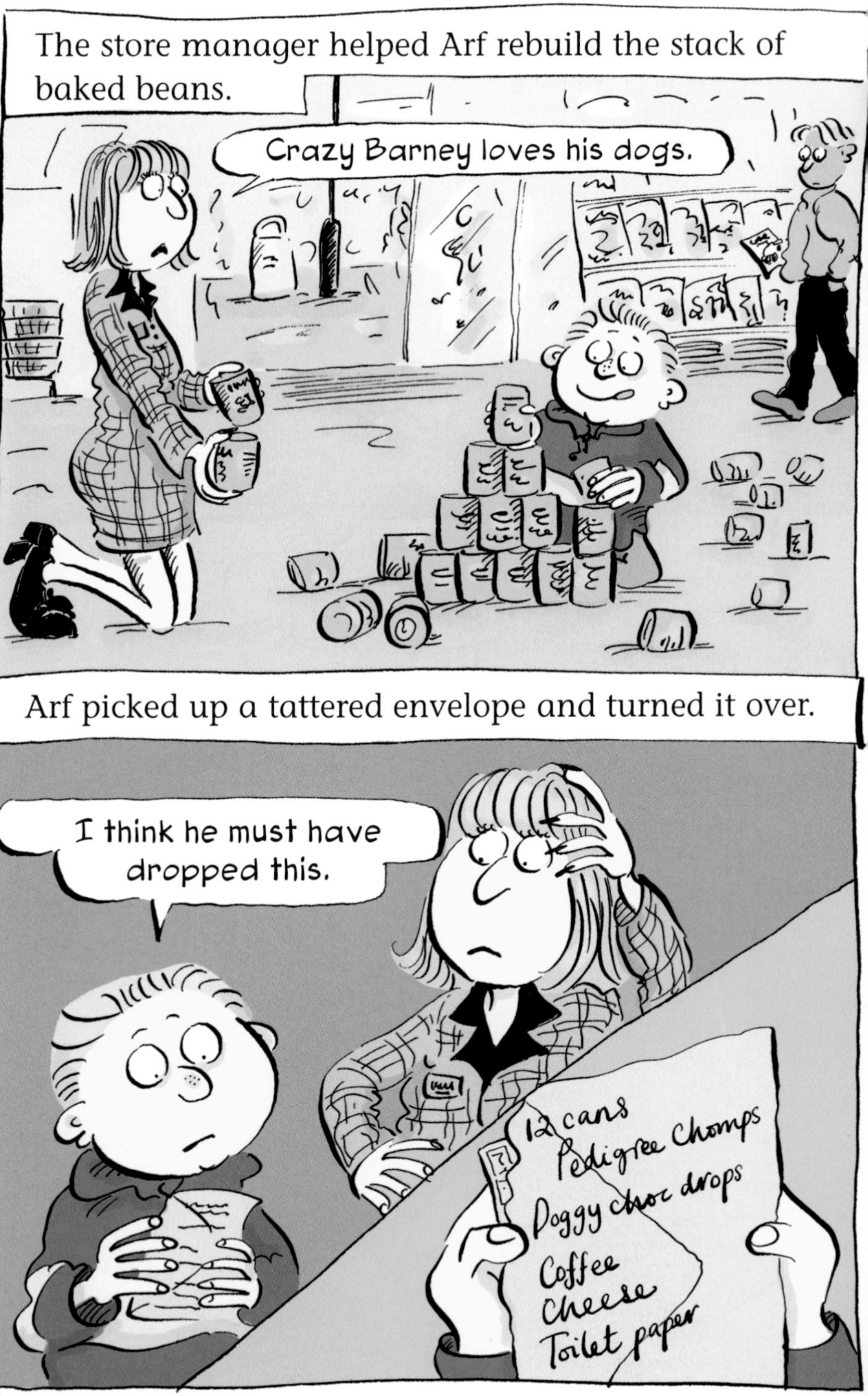
The store manager helped Arf rebuild the stack of baked beans.
Crazy Barney loves his dogs.
Arf picked up a tattered envelope and turned it over.
I think he must have dropped this.
12 cans
Pedigree Chomps
Doggy choc drops
Coffee
Cheese
Toilet paper

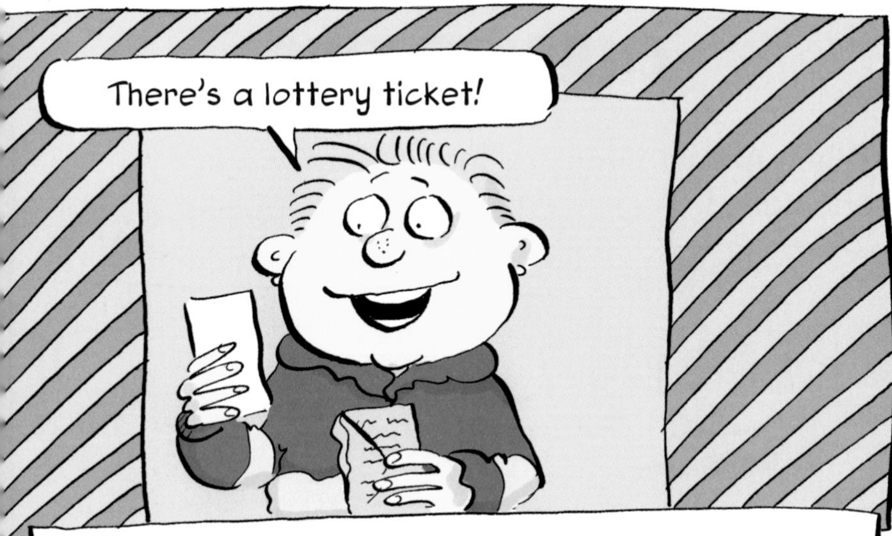
There's a lottery ticket!

Arf hurried out of the store. He looked left and right. Then left again. There was no sign of Barney.

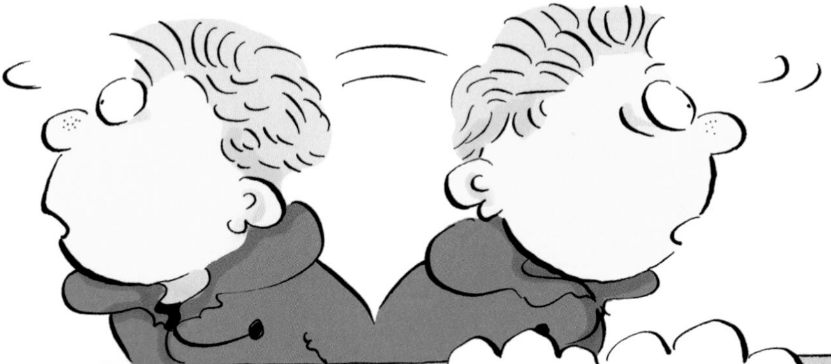

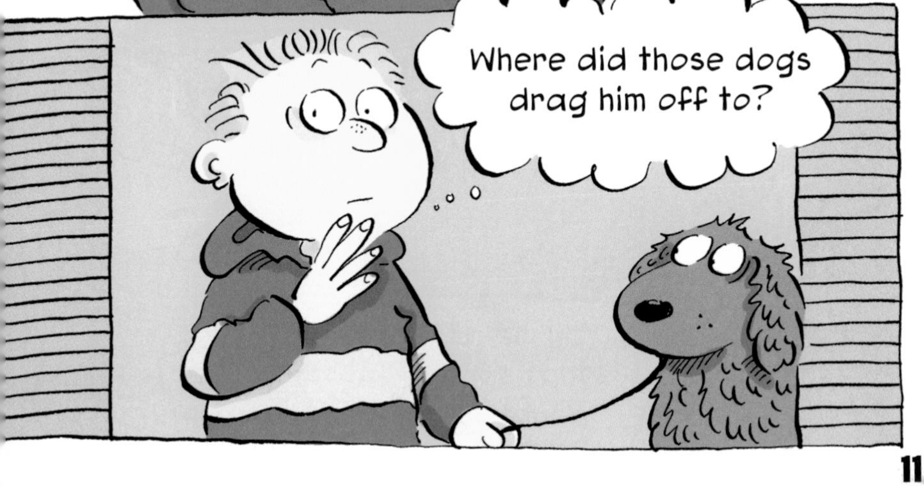
Where did those dogs drag him off to?

CHAPTER TWO

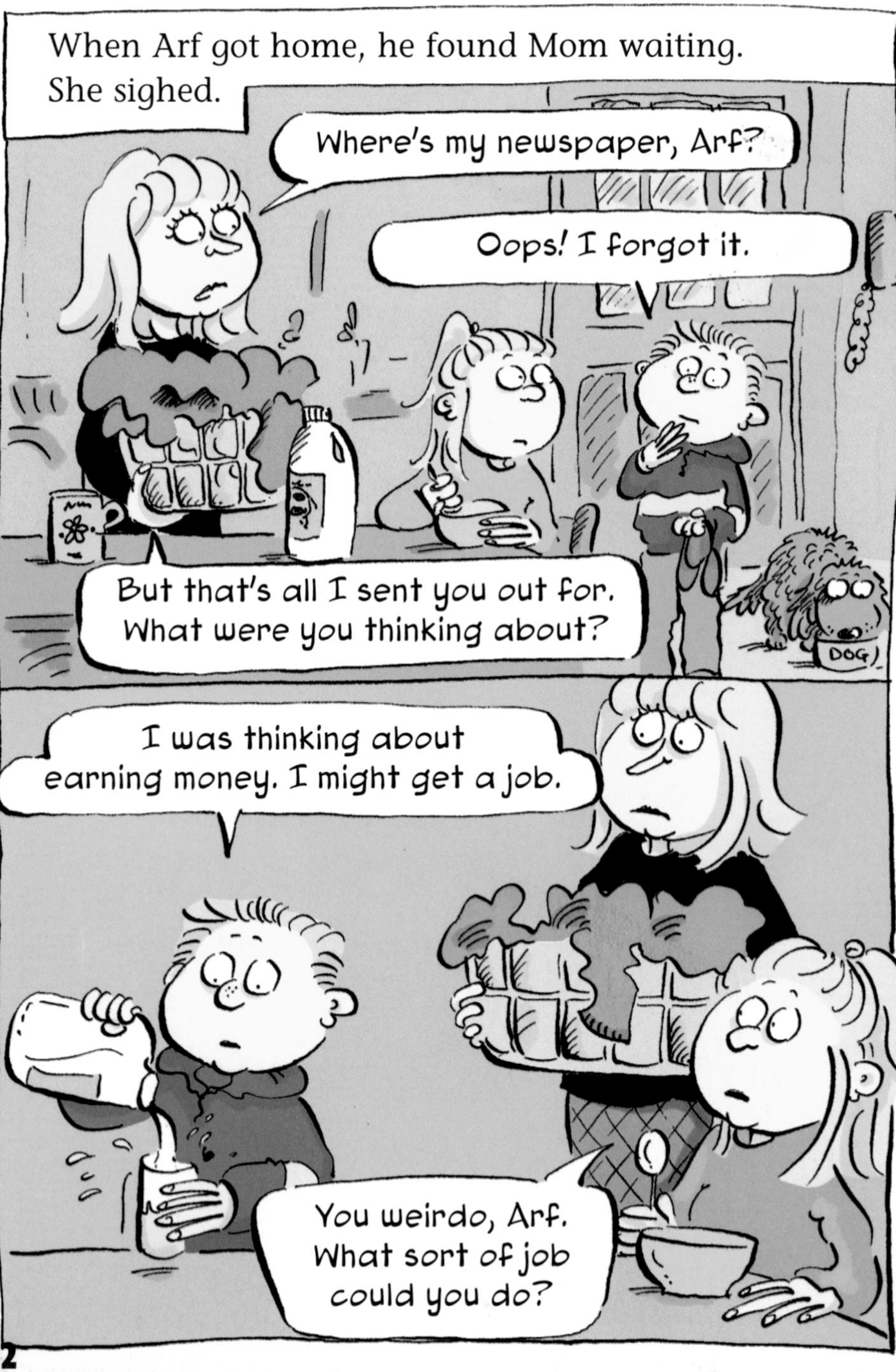
When Arf got home, he found Mom waiting. She sighed.
Where's my newspaper, Arf?
Oops! I forgot it.
But that's all I sent you out for. What were you thinking about?
DOG
I was thinking about earning money. I might get a job.
You weirdo, Arf. What sort of job could you do?

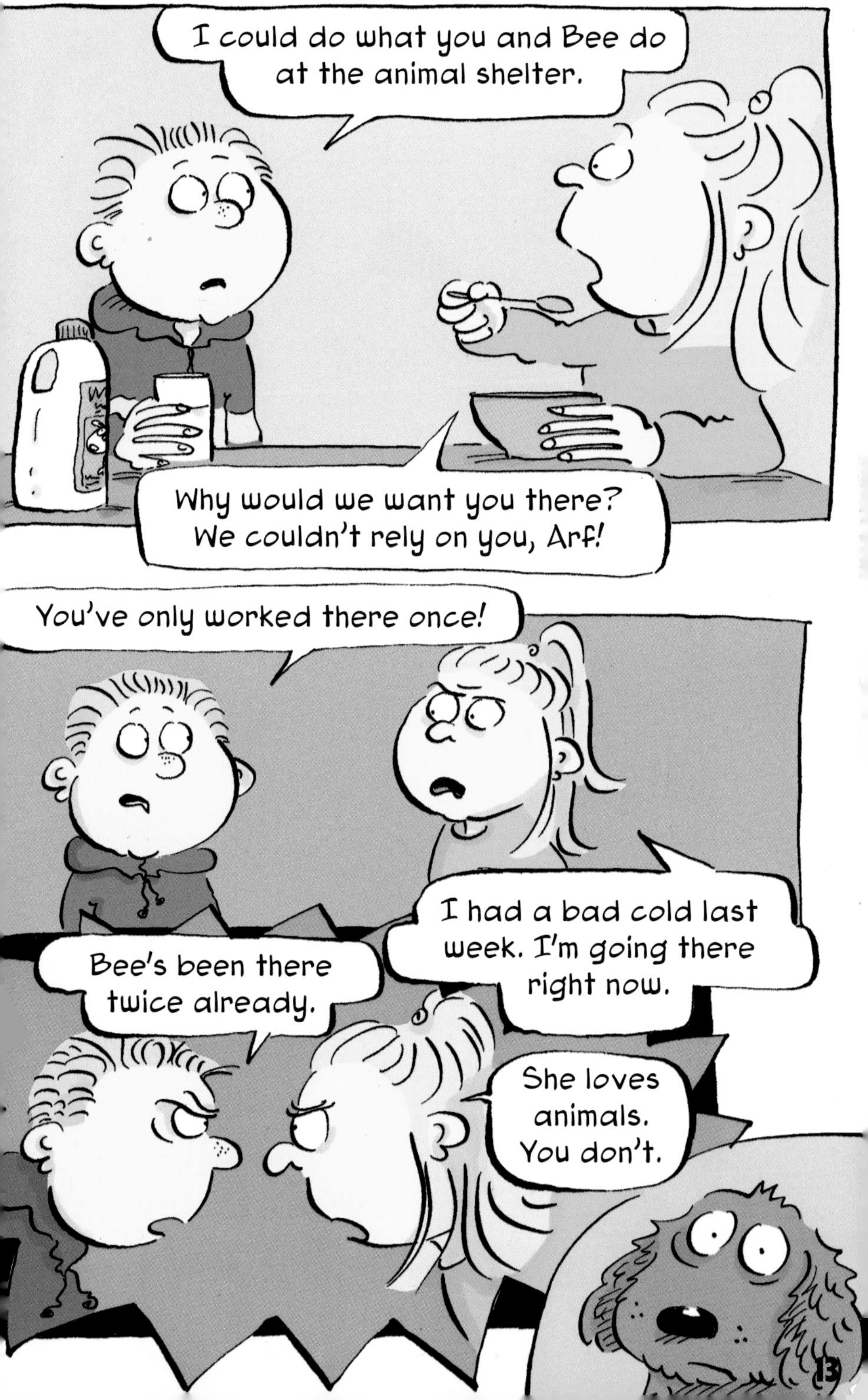
I could do what you and Bee do at the animal shelter.
Why would we want you there? We couldn't rely on you, Arf!
You've only worked there once!
I had a bad cold last week. I'm going there right now.
Bee's been there twice already.
She loves animals. You don't.

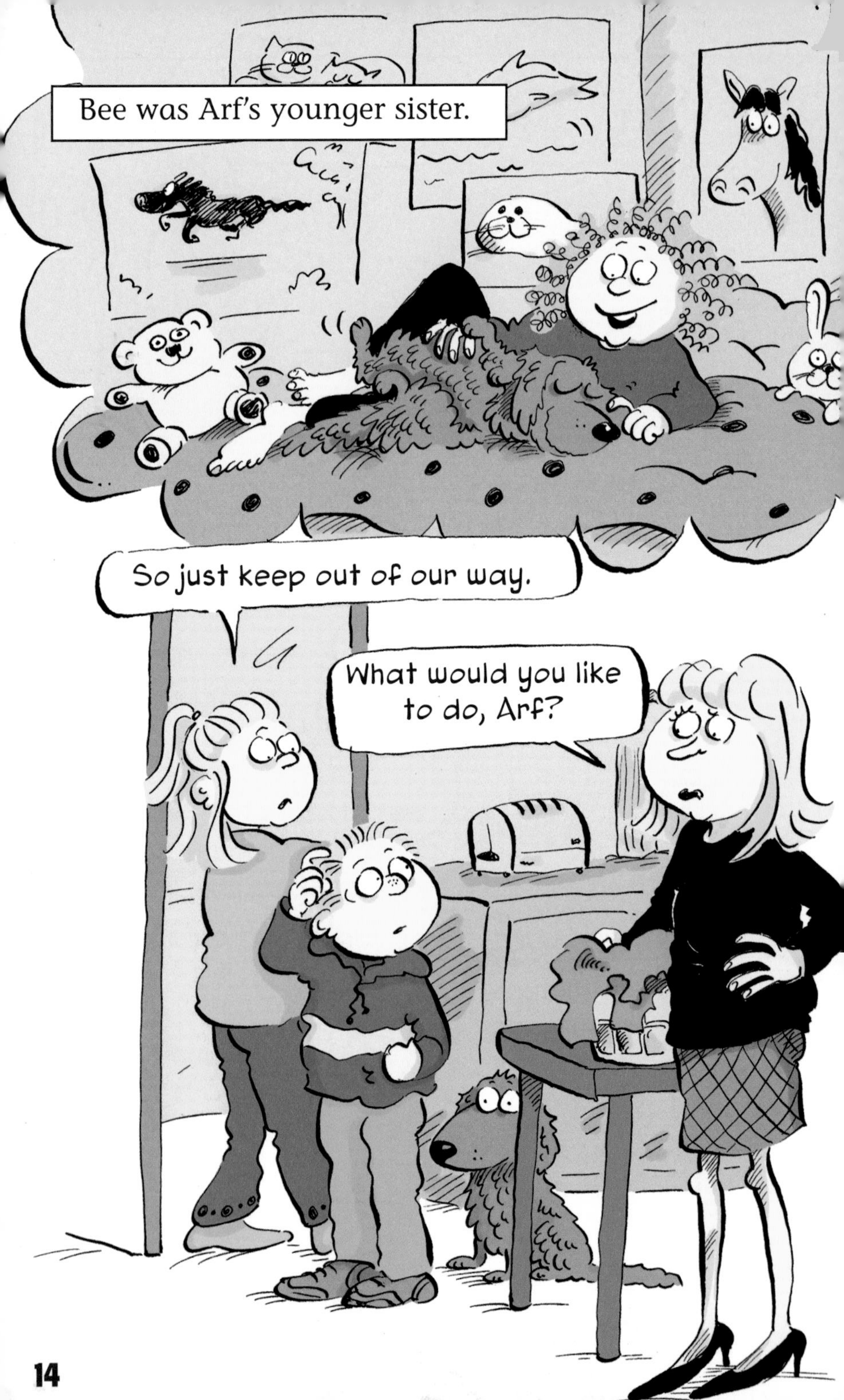

Bee was Arf's younger sister.
So just keep out of our way.
What would you like to do, Arf?

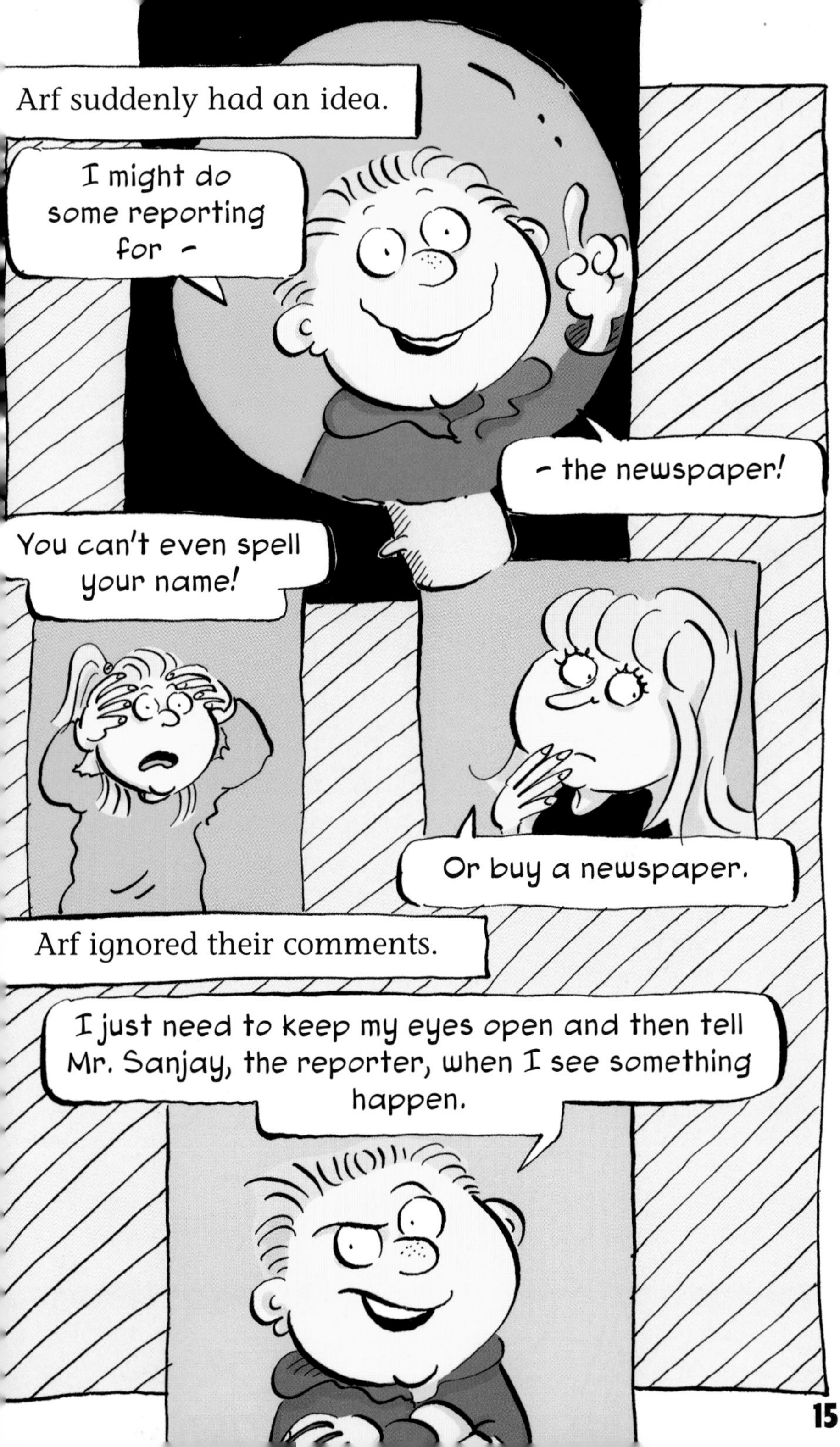
Arf suddenly had an idea.
I might do some reporting for -
- the newspaper!
You can't even spell your name!
Or buy a newspaper.
Arf ignored their comments.
I just need to keep my eyes open and then tell Mr. Sanjay, the reporter, when I see something happen.

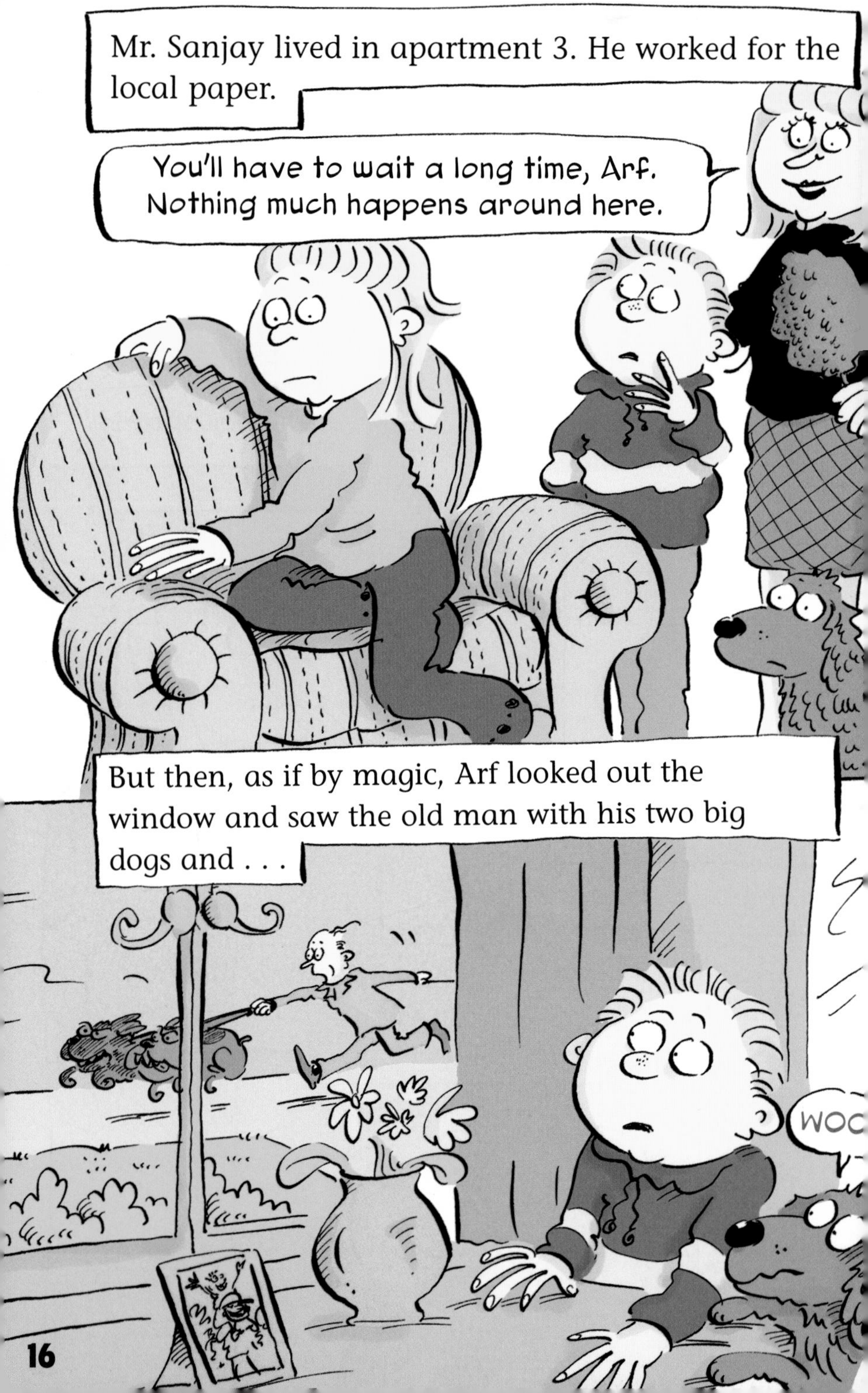
Mr. Sanjay lived in apartment 3. He worked for the local paper.
You'll have to wait a long time, Arf. Nothing much happens around here.
But then, as if by magic, Arf looked out the window and saw the old man with his two big dogs and . . .

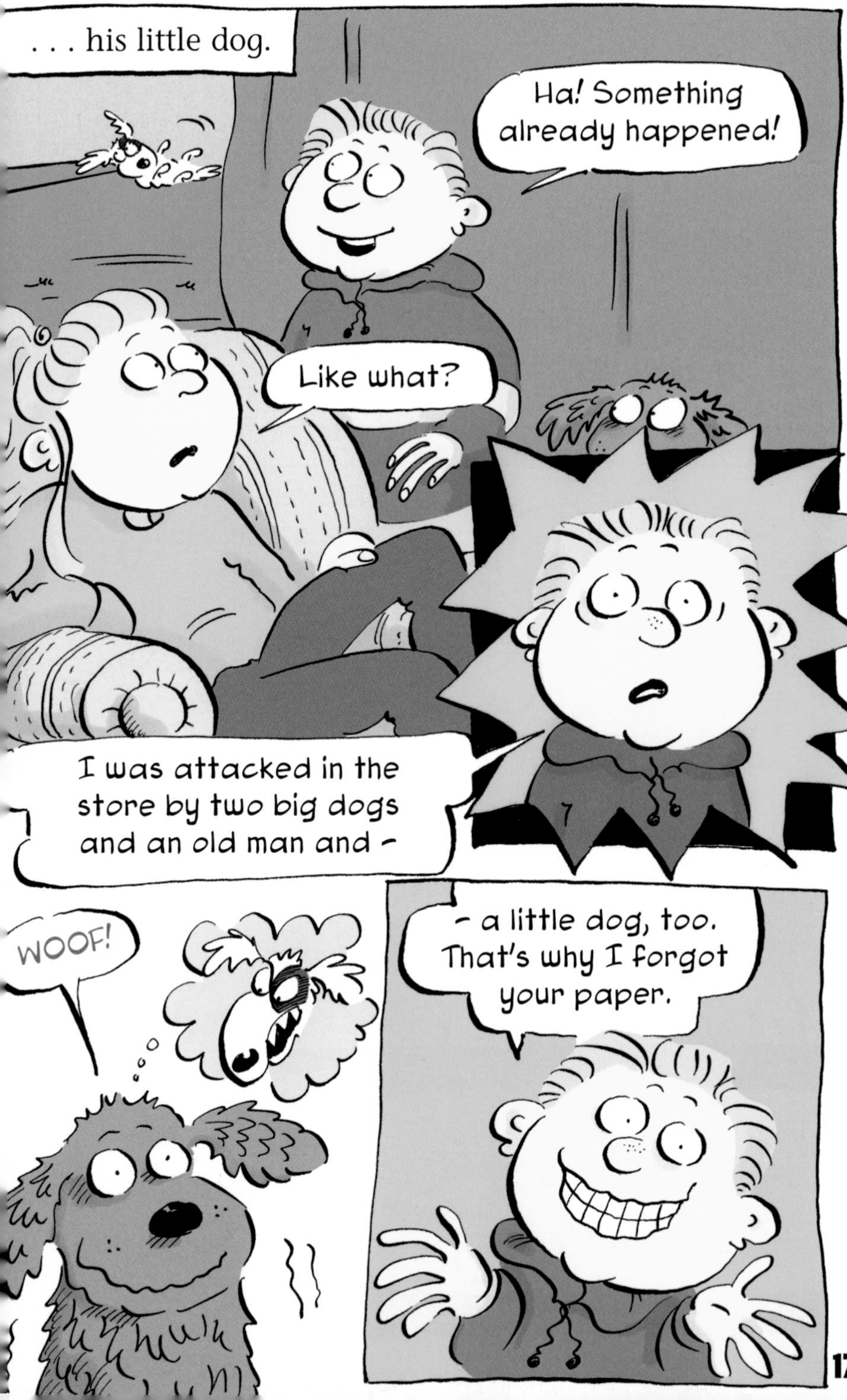
. . . his little dog.
Ha! Something already happened!
Like what?
I was attacked in the store by two big dogs and an old man and -
WOOF!
- a little dog, too. That's why I forgot your paper.

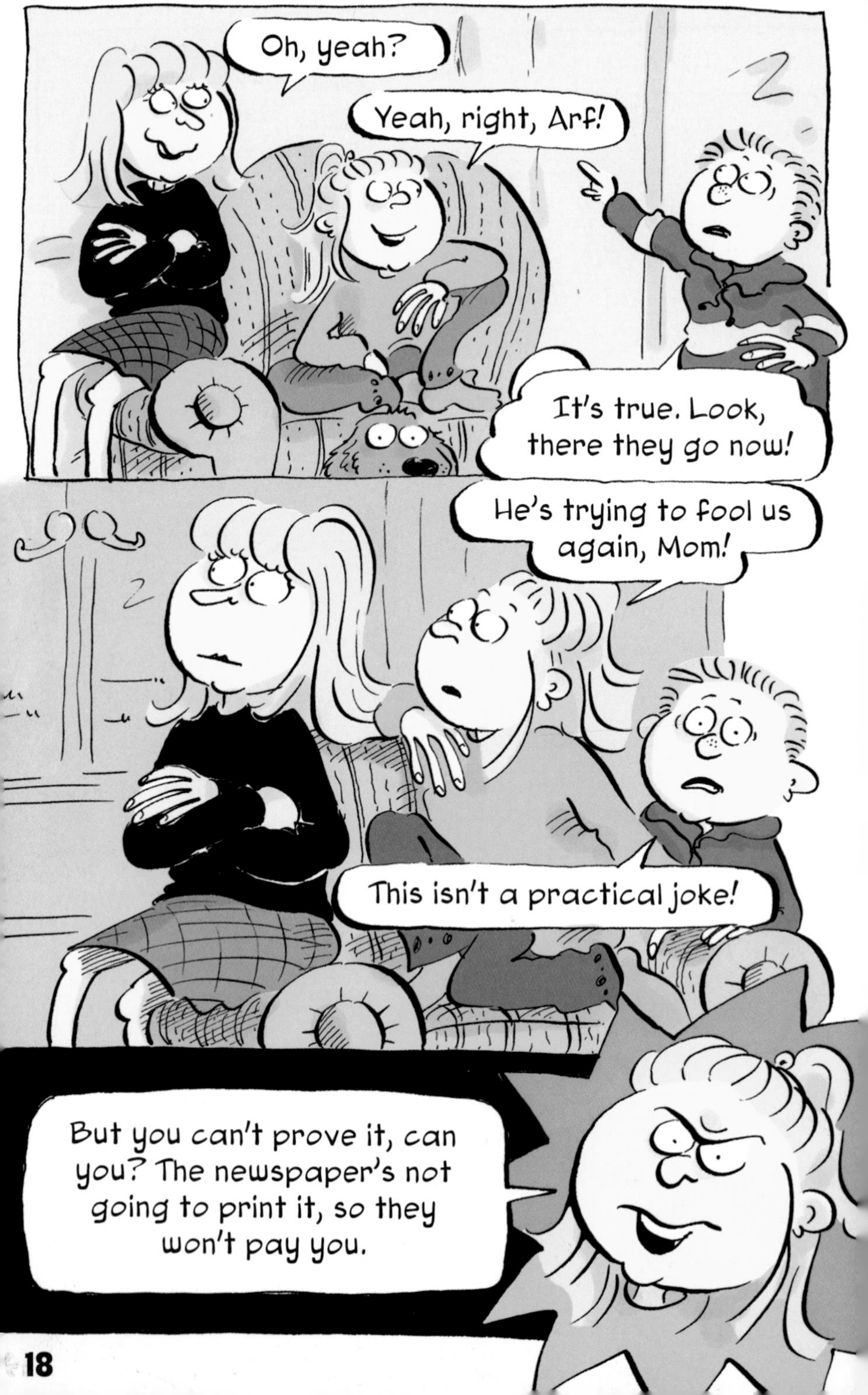
Oh, yeah?
Yeah, right, Arf!
It's true. Look, there they go now!
He's trying to fool us again, Mom!
This isn't a practical joke!
But you can't prove it, can you? The newspaper's not going to print it, so they won't pay you.

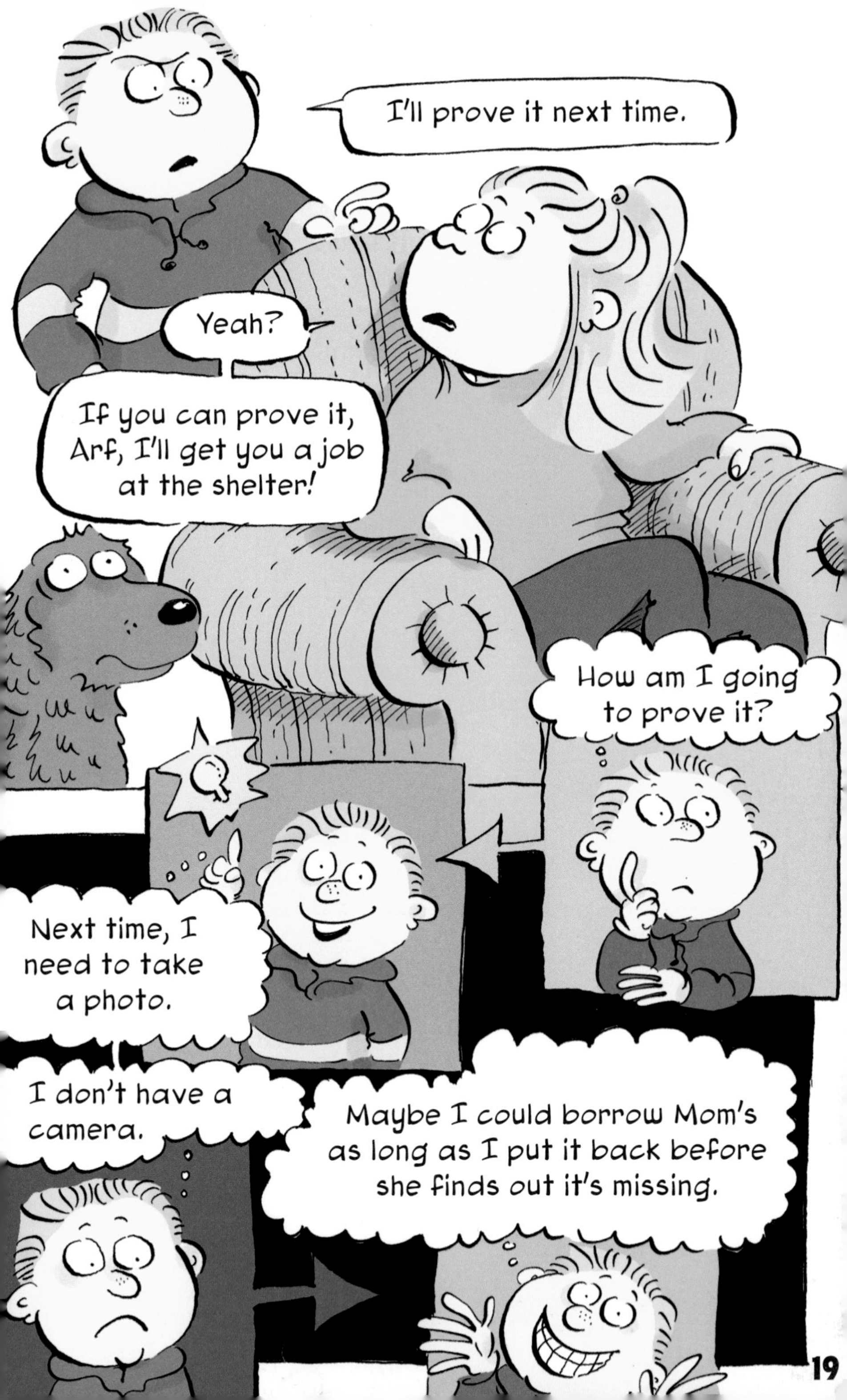
I'll prove it next time.
Yeah?
If you can prove it, Arf, I'll get you a job at the shelter!
How am I going to prove it?
Next time, I need to take a photo.
I don't have a camera.
Maybe I could borrow Mom's as long as I put it back before she finds out it's missing.

CHAPTER THREE

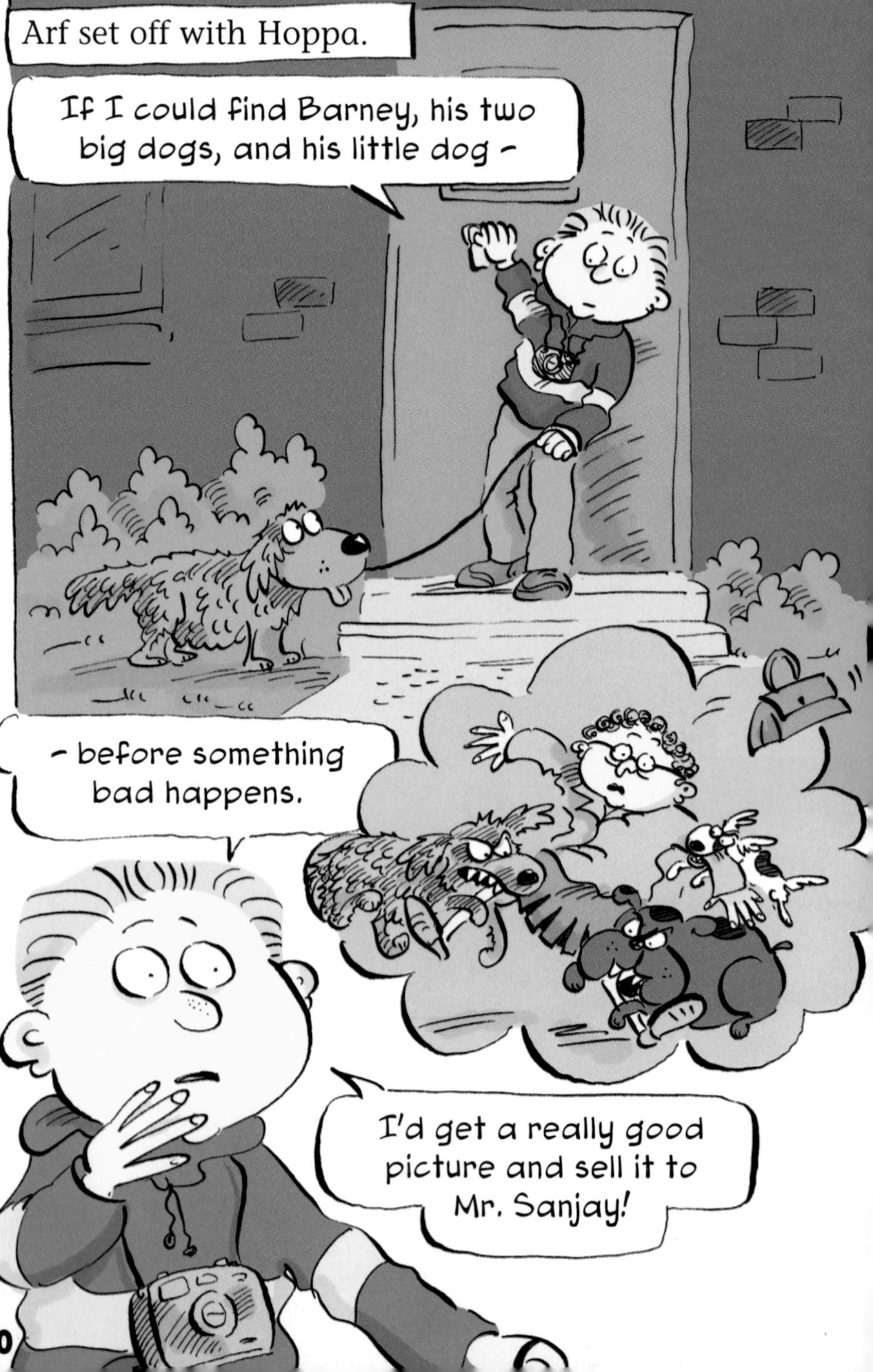
Arf set off with Hoppa.
If I could find Barney, his two big dogs, and his little dog –
– before something bad happens.
I'd get a really good picture and sell it to Mr. Sanjay!

But Arf walked up and down the streets for more than half an hour without finding Crazy Barney.

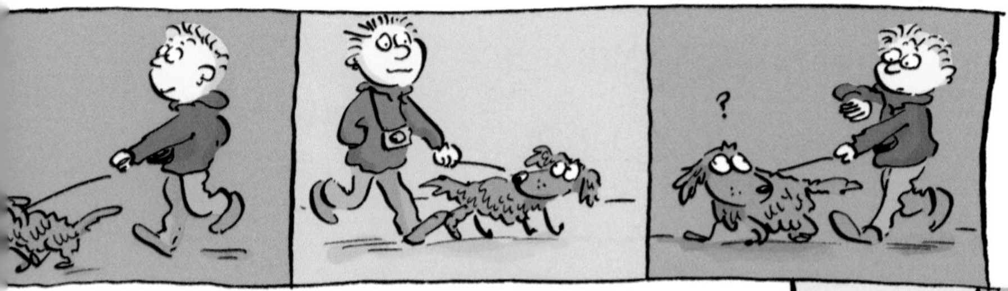

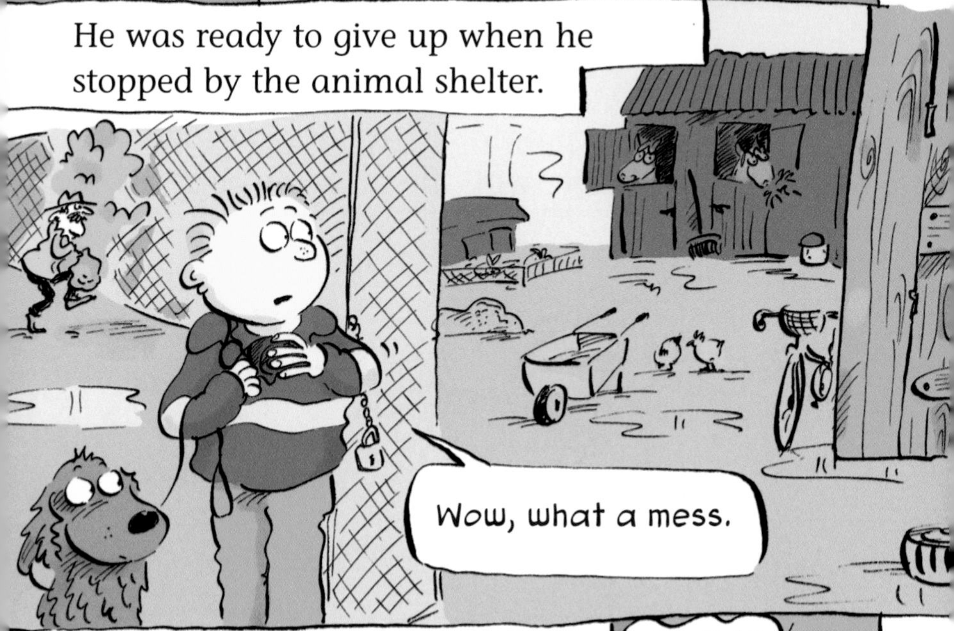
He was ready to give up when he stopped by the animal shelter.
Wow, what a mess.

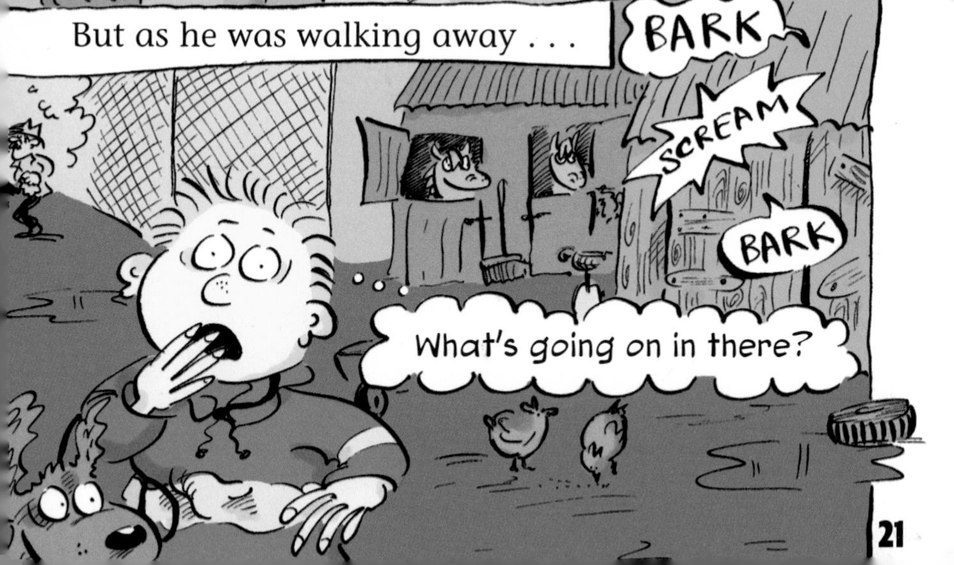
But as he was walking away . . .
BARK
SCREAM
BARK
What's going on in there?

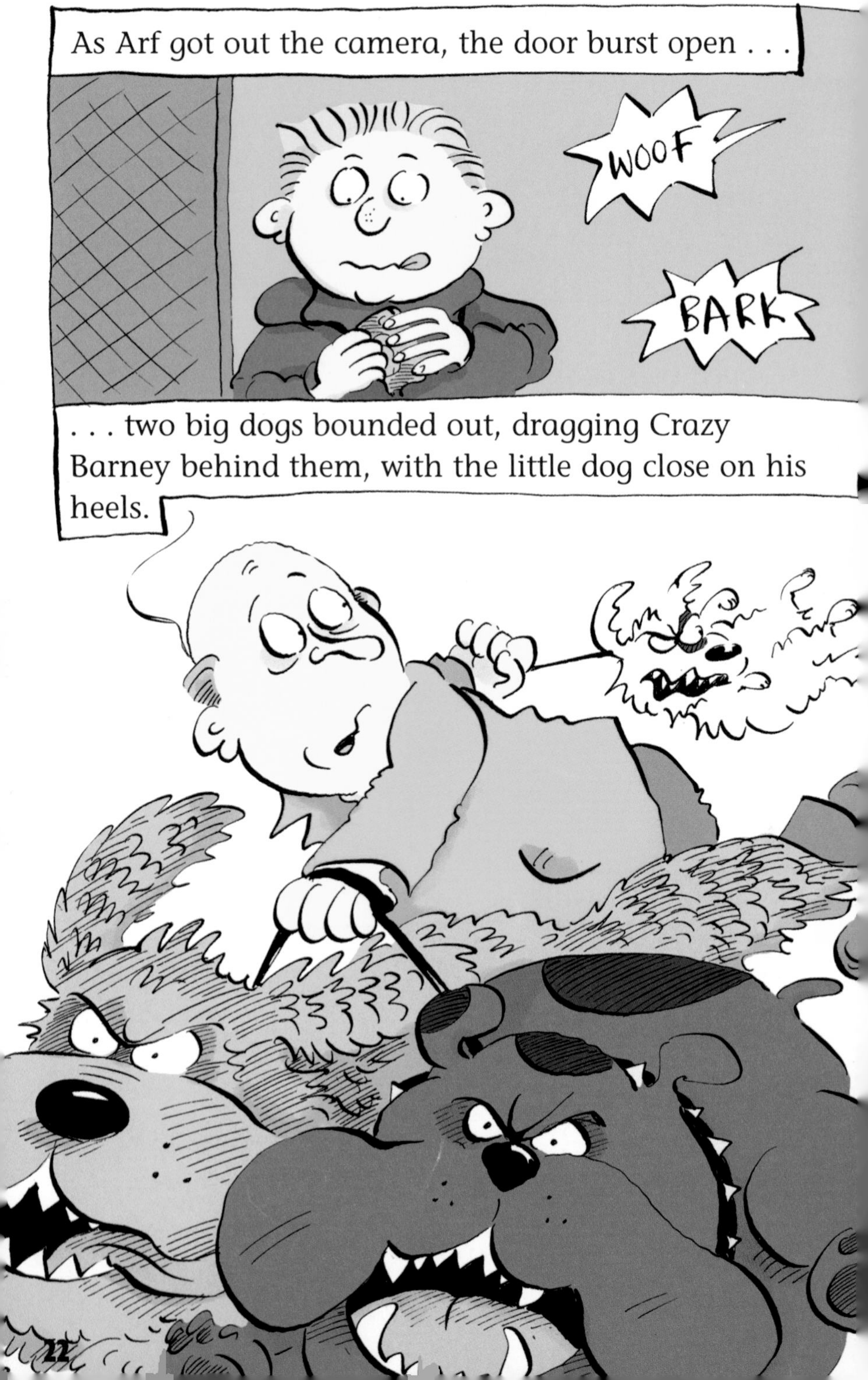
As Arf got out the camera, the door burst open . . .
WOOF
BARK
. . . two big dogs bounded out, dragging Crazy Barney behind them, with the little dog close on his heels.

Arf managed to snap three pictures before he was knocked off his feet by the dogs.

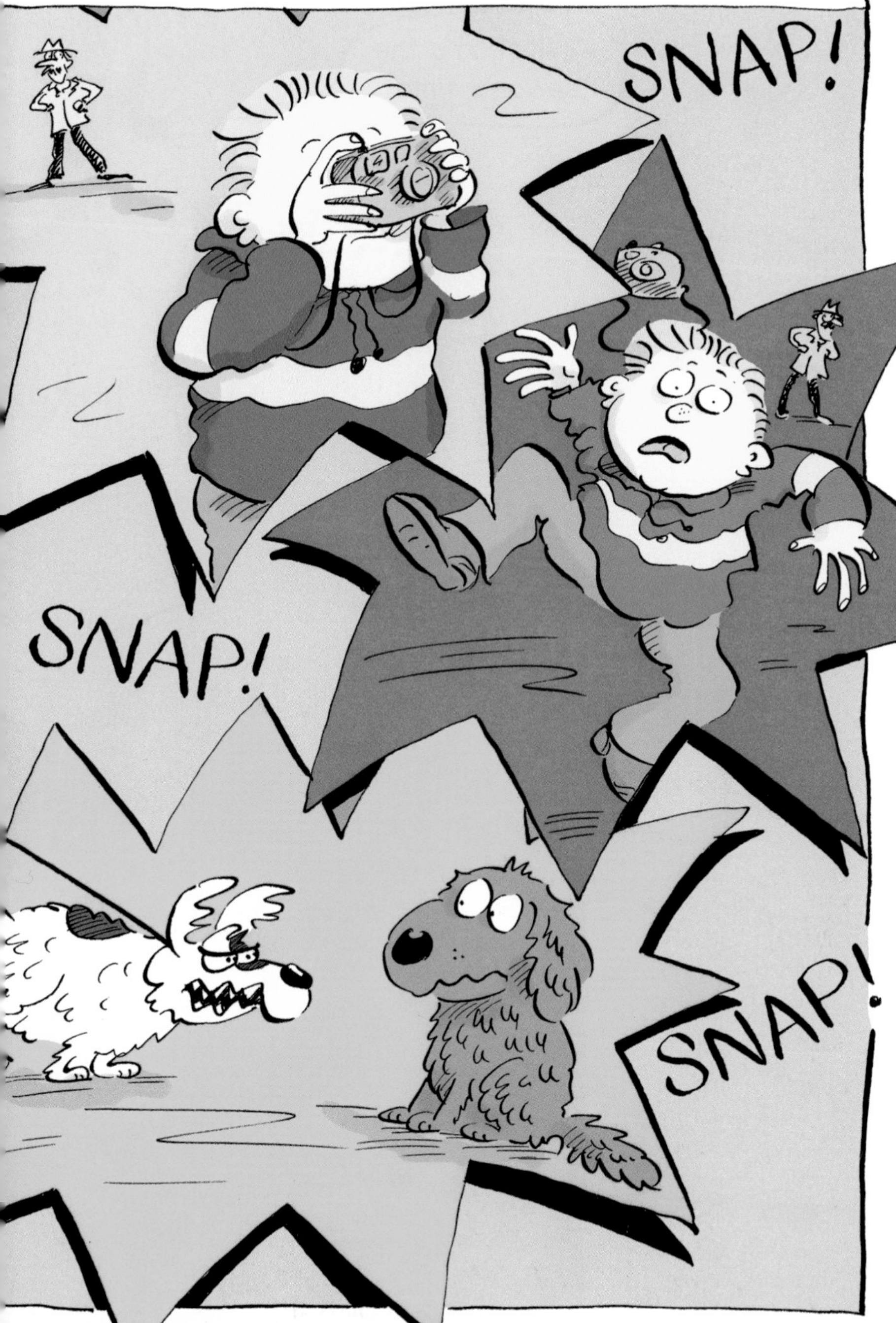
SNAP!
SNAP!
SNAP!

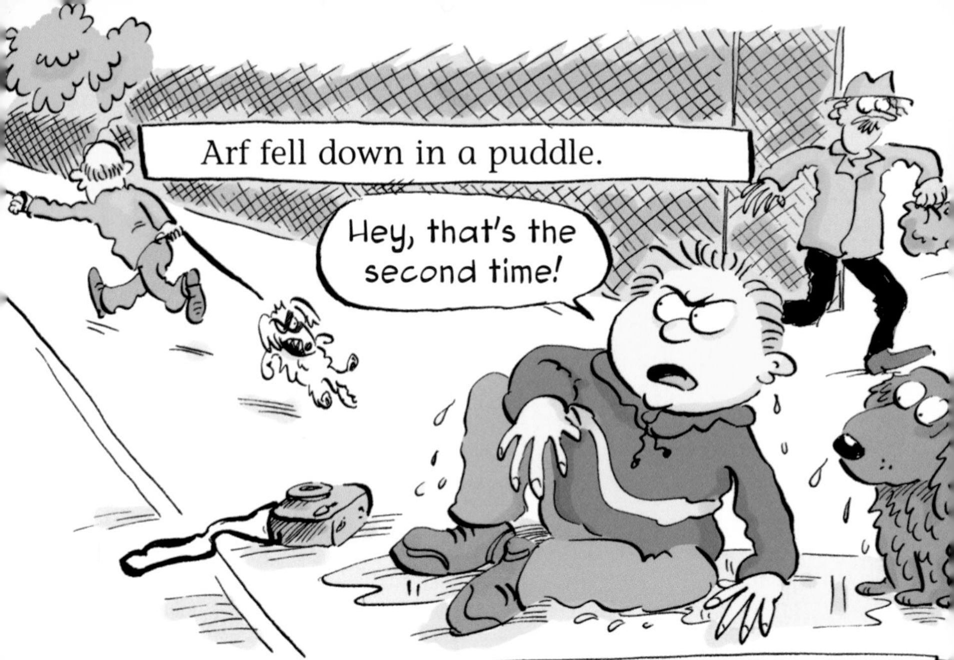
Arf fell down in a puddle.
Hey, that's the second time!

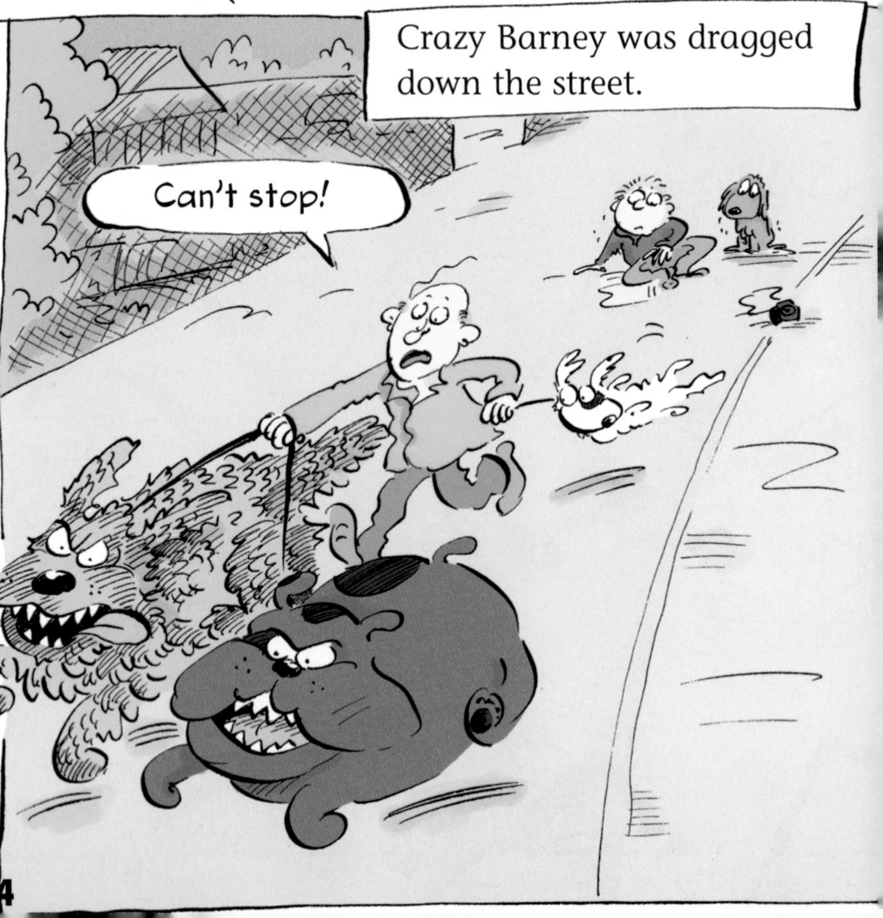
Crazy Barney was dragged down the street.
Can't stop!

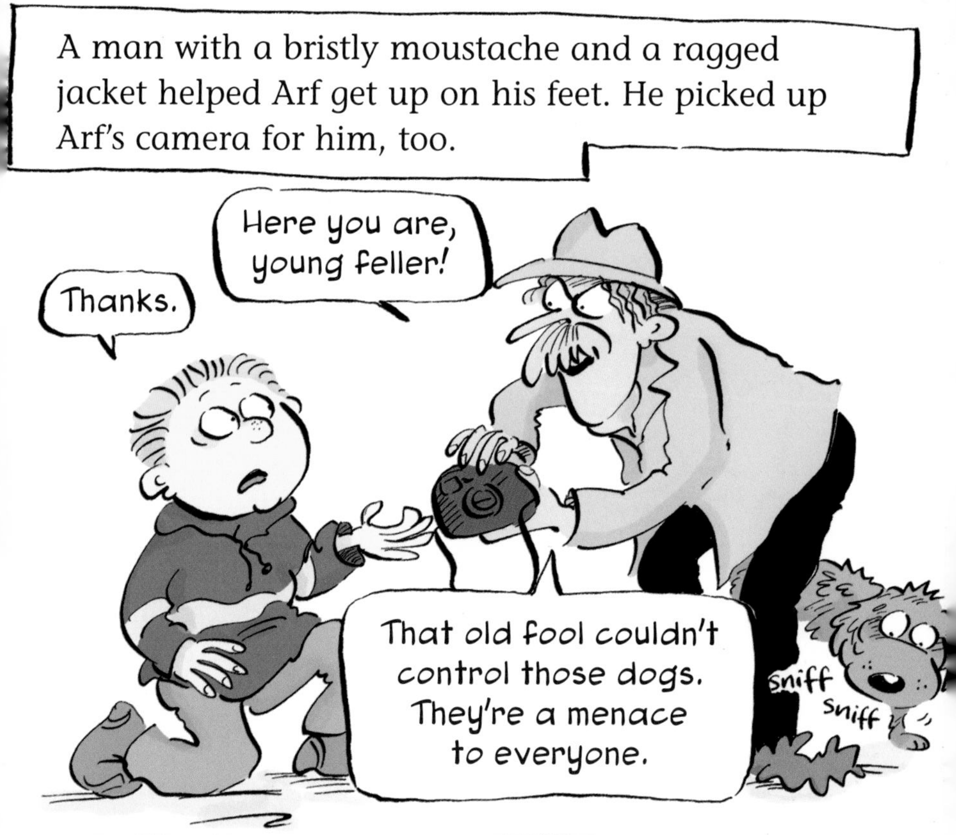
A man with a bristly moustache and a ragged jacket helped Arf get up on his feet. He picked up Arf's camera for him, too.
Thanks.
Here you are, young feller!
That old fool couldn't control those dogs. They're a menace to everyone.
sniff
sniff

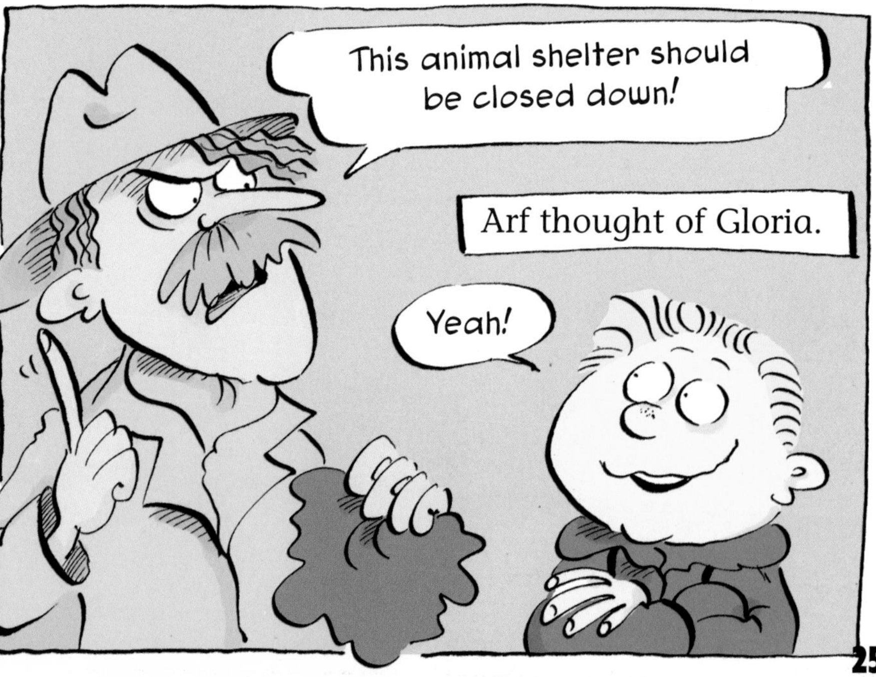
This animal shelter should be closed down!
Arf thought of Gloria.
Yeah!

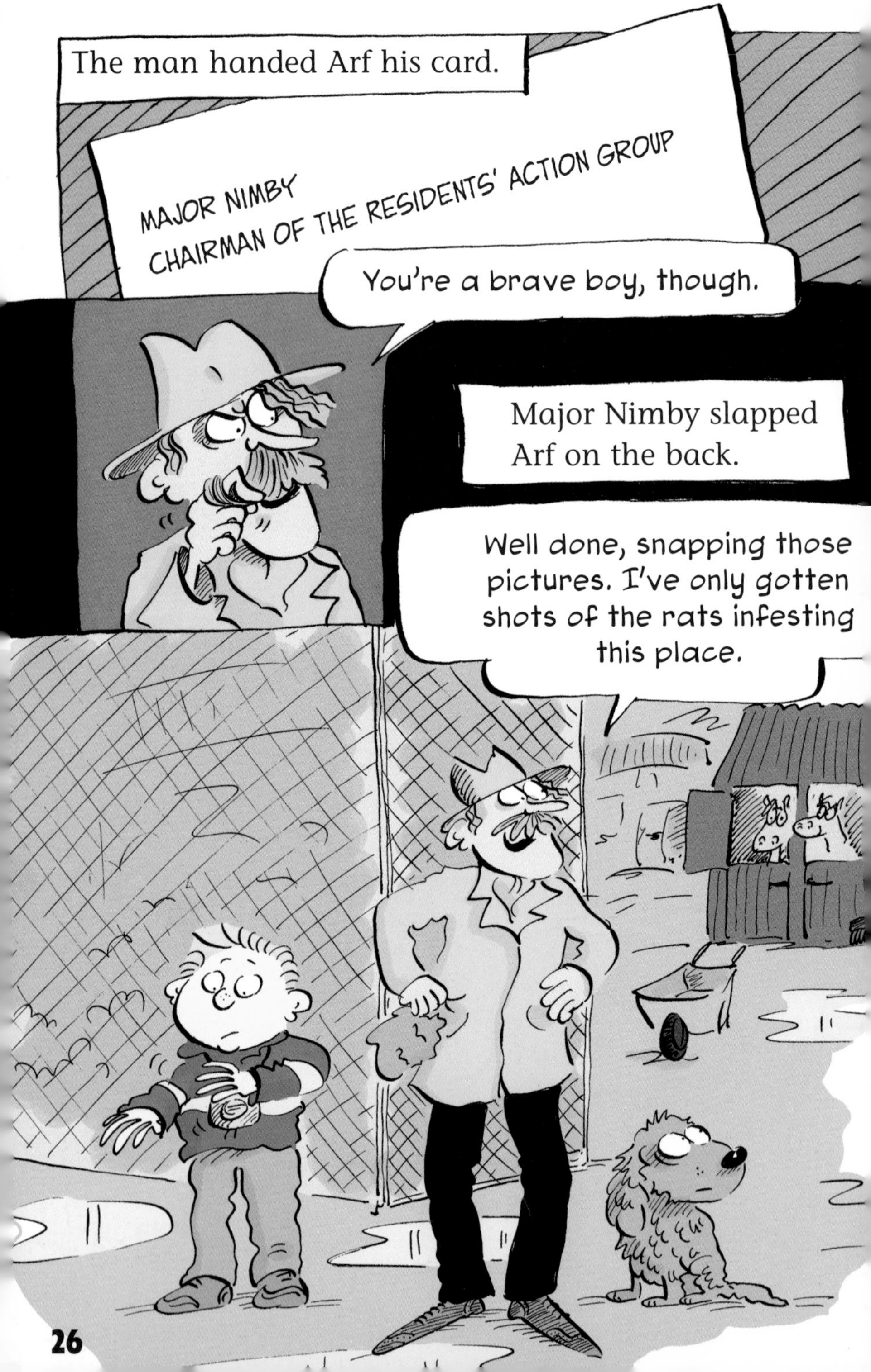
The man handed Arf his card.
MAJOR NIMBY
CHAIRMAN OF THE RESIDENTS' ACTION GROUP
You're a brave boy, though.
Major Nimby slapped Arf on the back.
Well done, snapping those pictures. I've only gotten shots of the rats infesting this place.

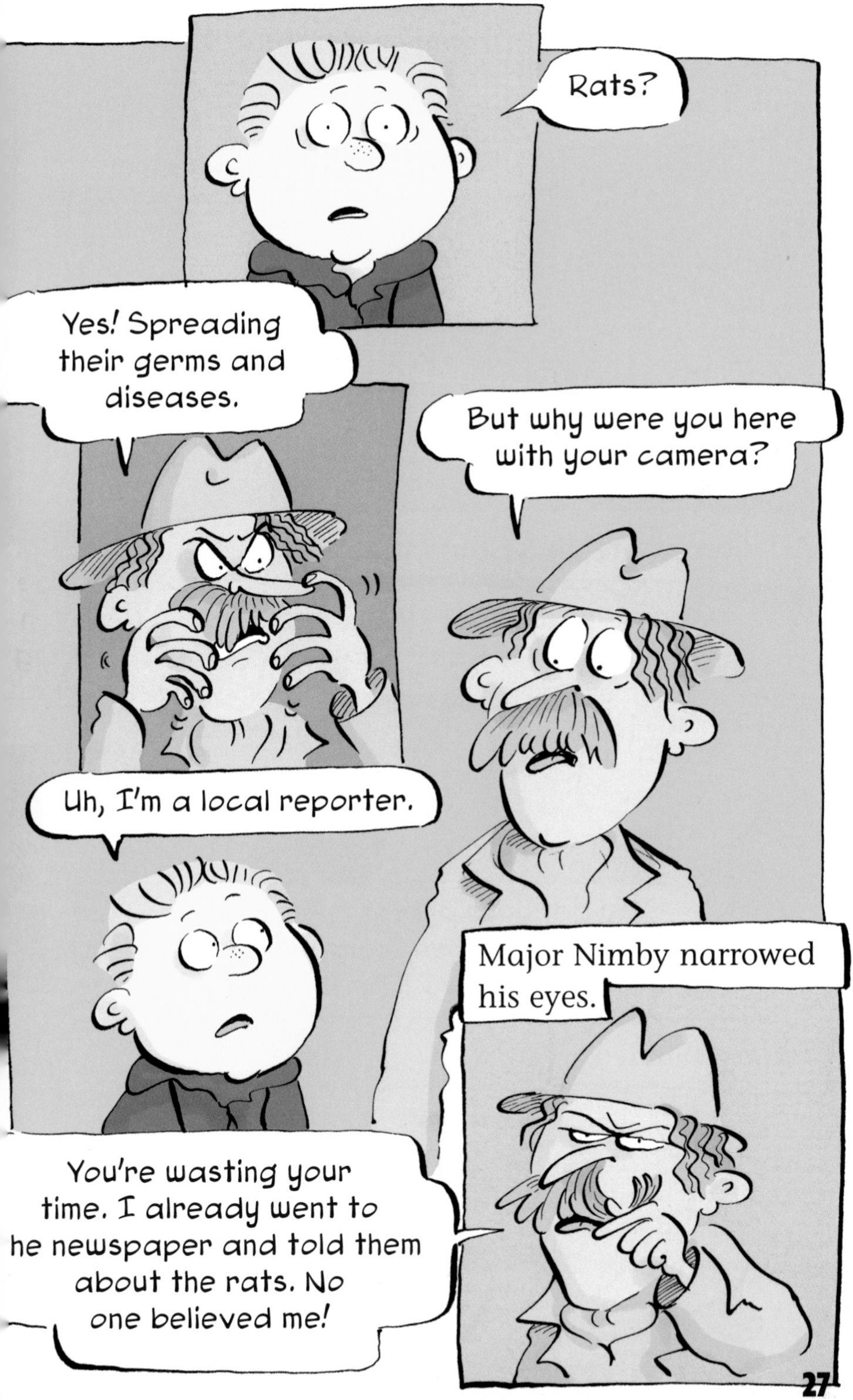
Rats?
Yes! Spreading their germs and diseases.
But why were you here with your camera?
Uh, I'm a local reporter.
Major Nimby narrowed his eyes.
You're wasting your time. I already went to he newspaper and told them about the rats. No one believed me!

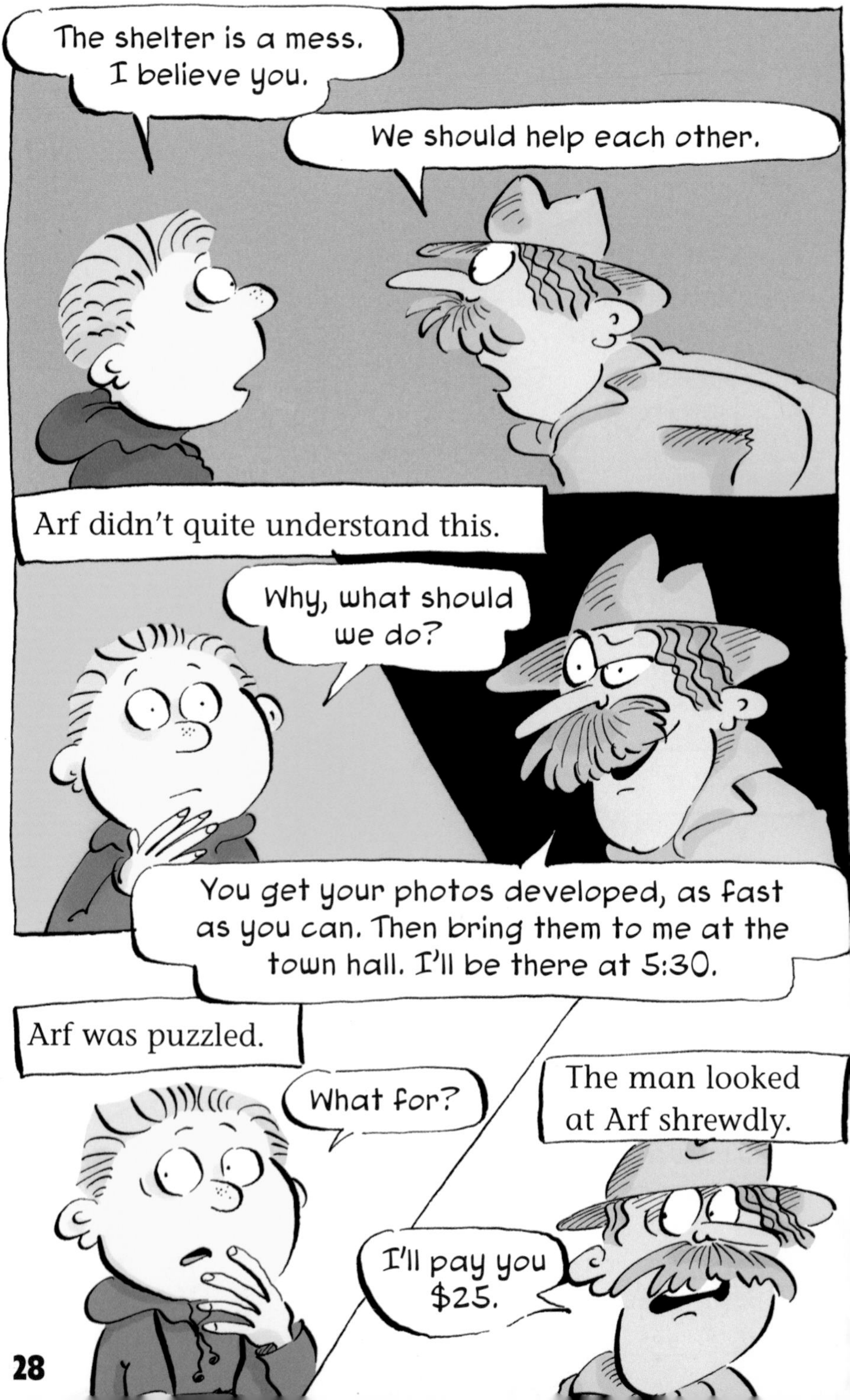
The shelter is a mess. I believe you.
We should help each other.
Arf didn't quite understand this.
Why, what should we do?
You get your photos developed, as fast as you can. Then bring them to me at the town hall. I'll be there at 5:30.
Arf was puzzled.
What for?
The man looked at Arf shrewdly.
I'll pay you $25.

CHAPTER FOUR

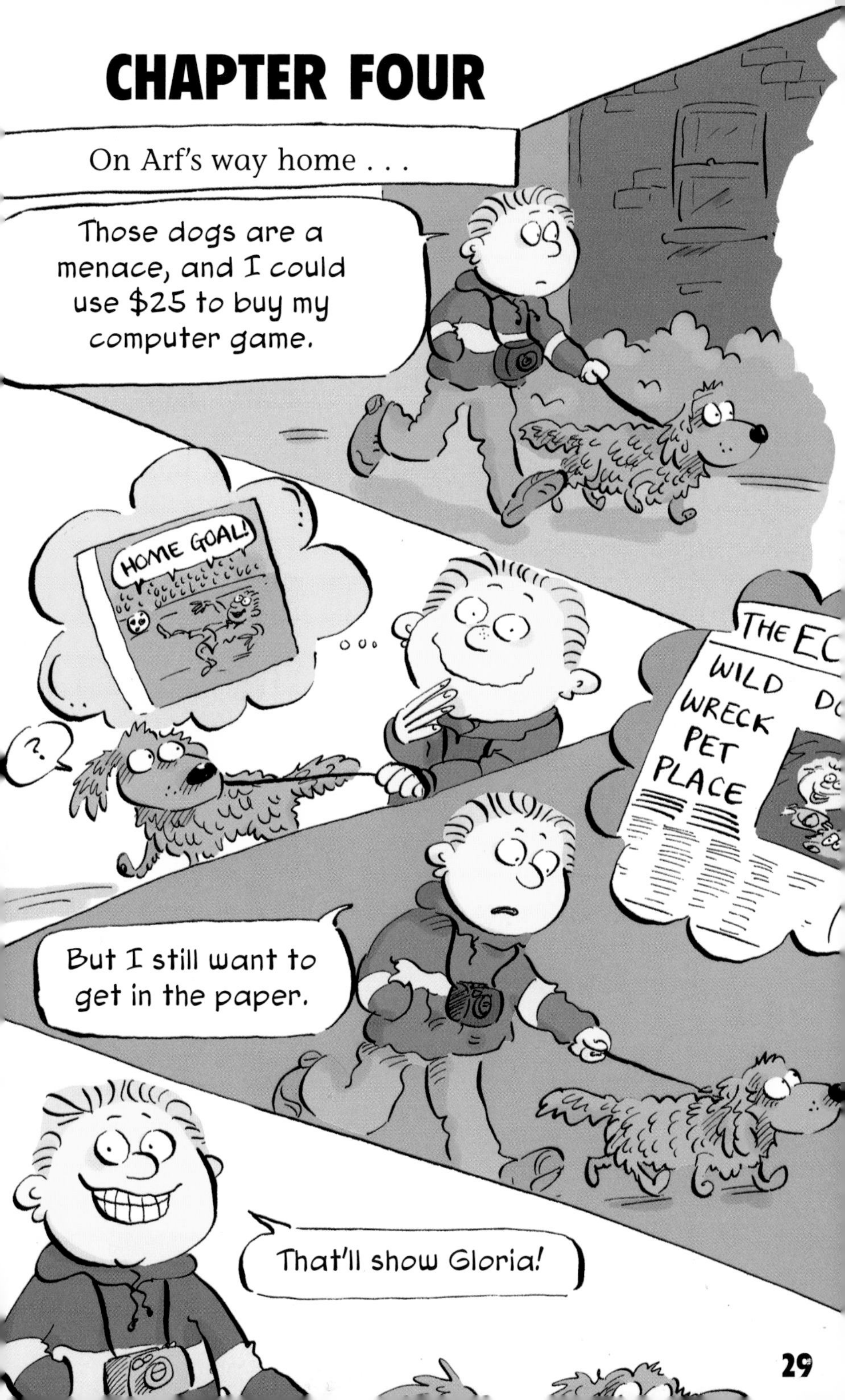

On Arf's way home . . .
Those dogs are a menace, and I could use $25 to buy my computer game.
HOME GOAL!
?
WILD
WRECK PET PLACE
But I still want to get in the paper.
That'll show Gloria!

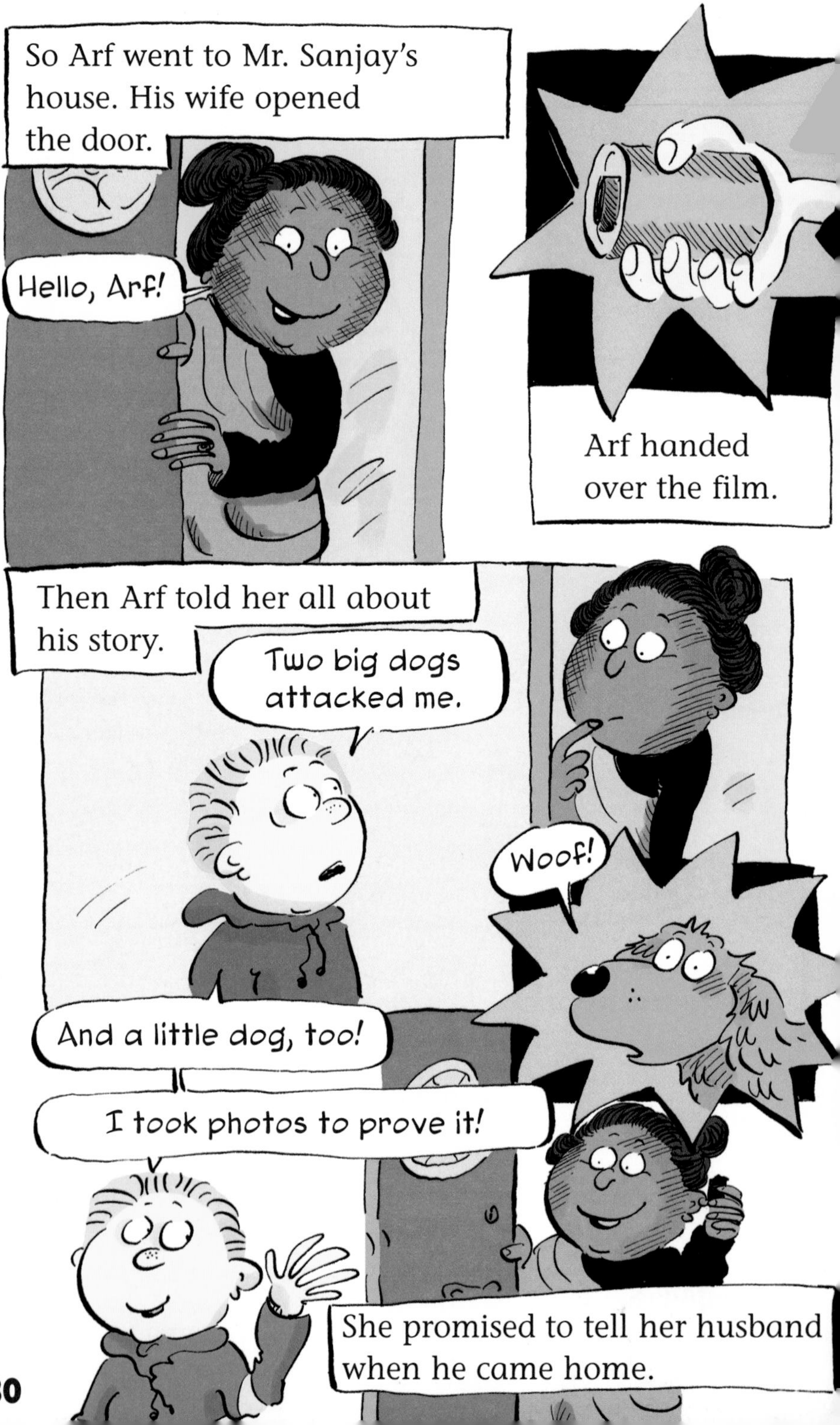
So Arf went to Mr. Sanjay's house. His wife opened the door.
Hello, Arf!
Arf handed over the film.
Then Arf told her all about his story.
Two big dogs attacked me.
Woof!
And a little dog, too!
I took photos to prove it!
She promised to tell her husband when he came home.

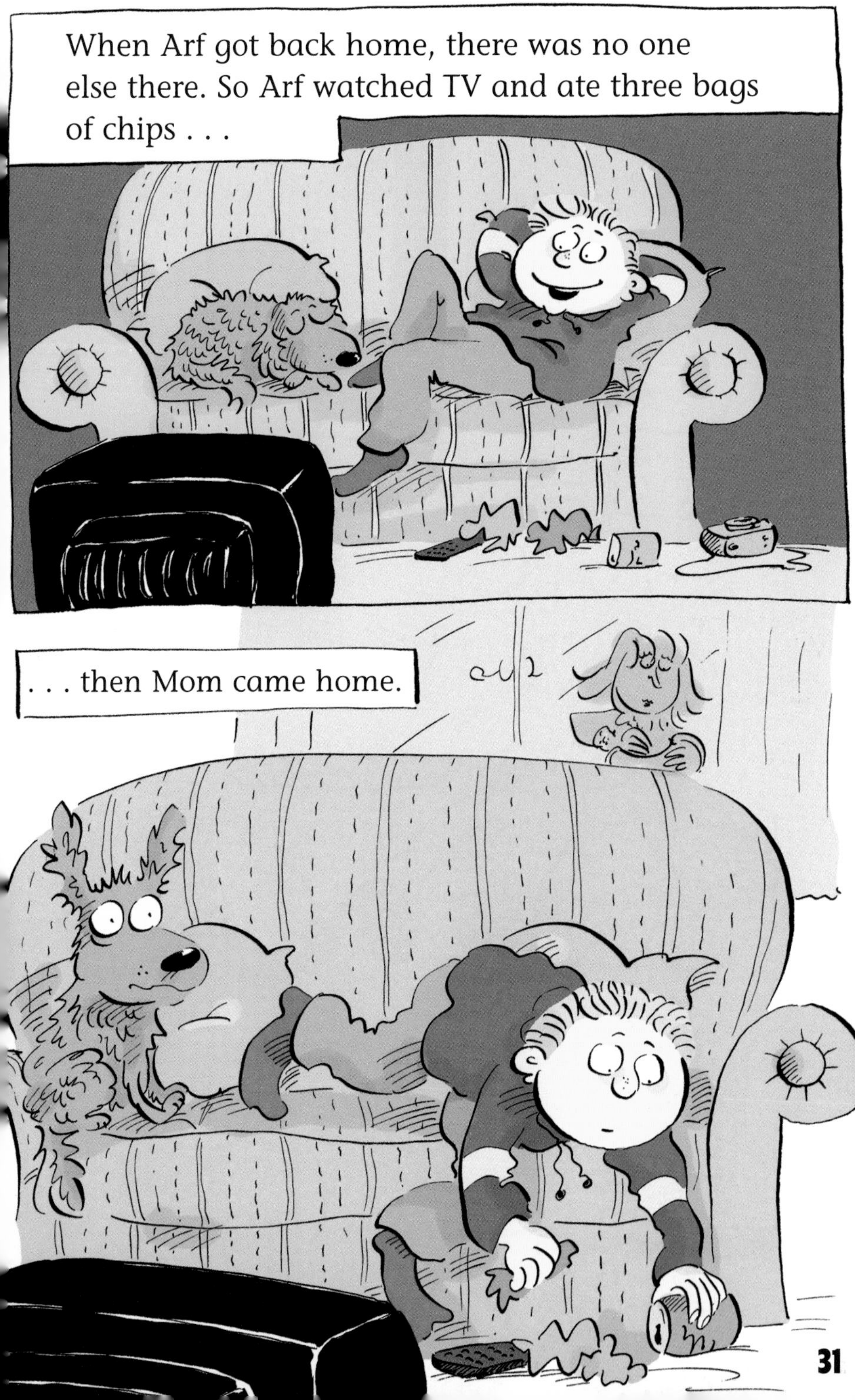
When Arf got back home, there was no one else there. So Arf watched TV and ate three bags of chips . . .
. . . then Mom came home.

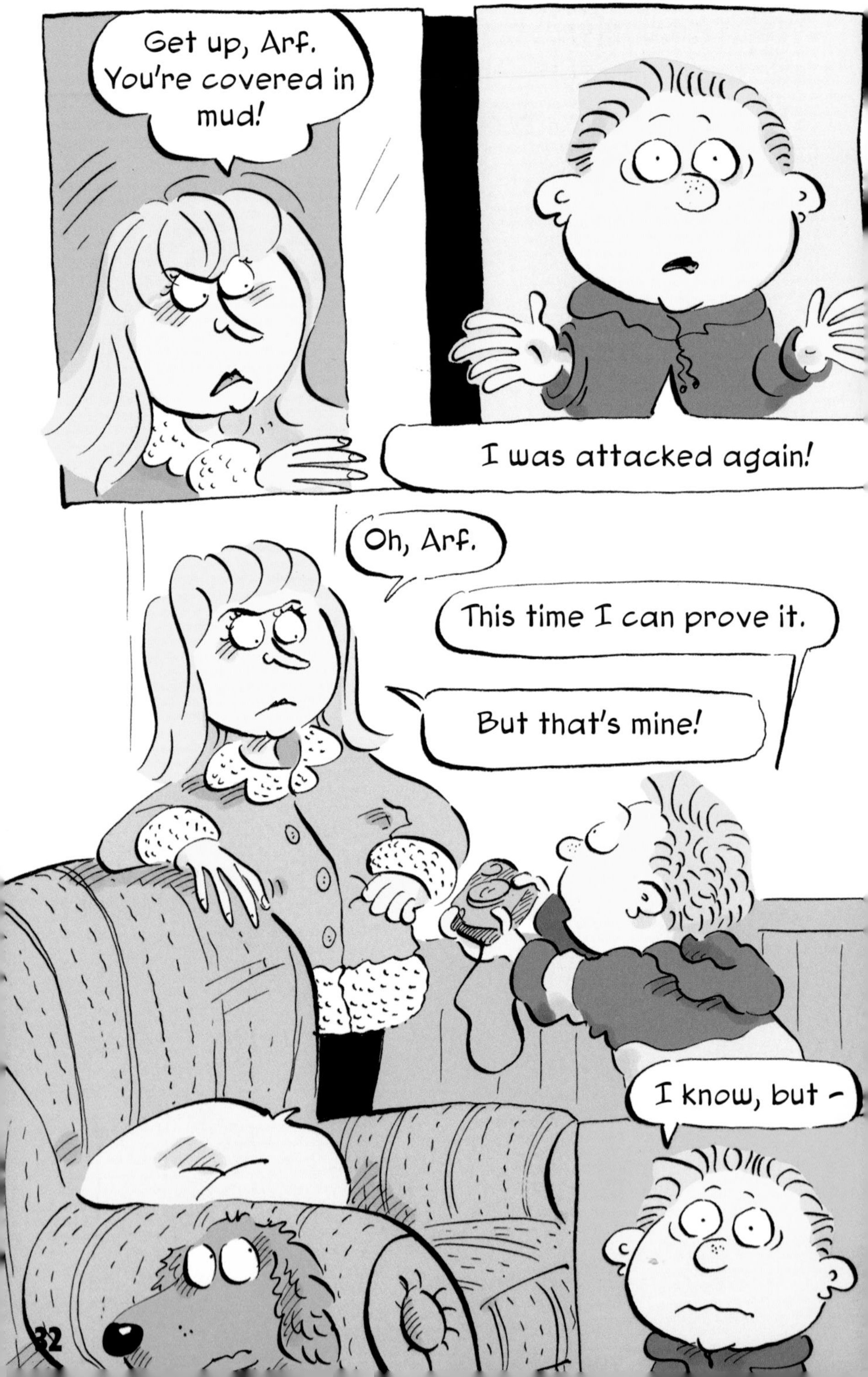
Get up, Arf. You're covered in mud!
I was attacked again!
Oh, Arf.
This time I can prove it.
But that's mine!
I know, but -

Before Arf could explain, there was a knock on the door.

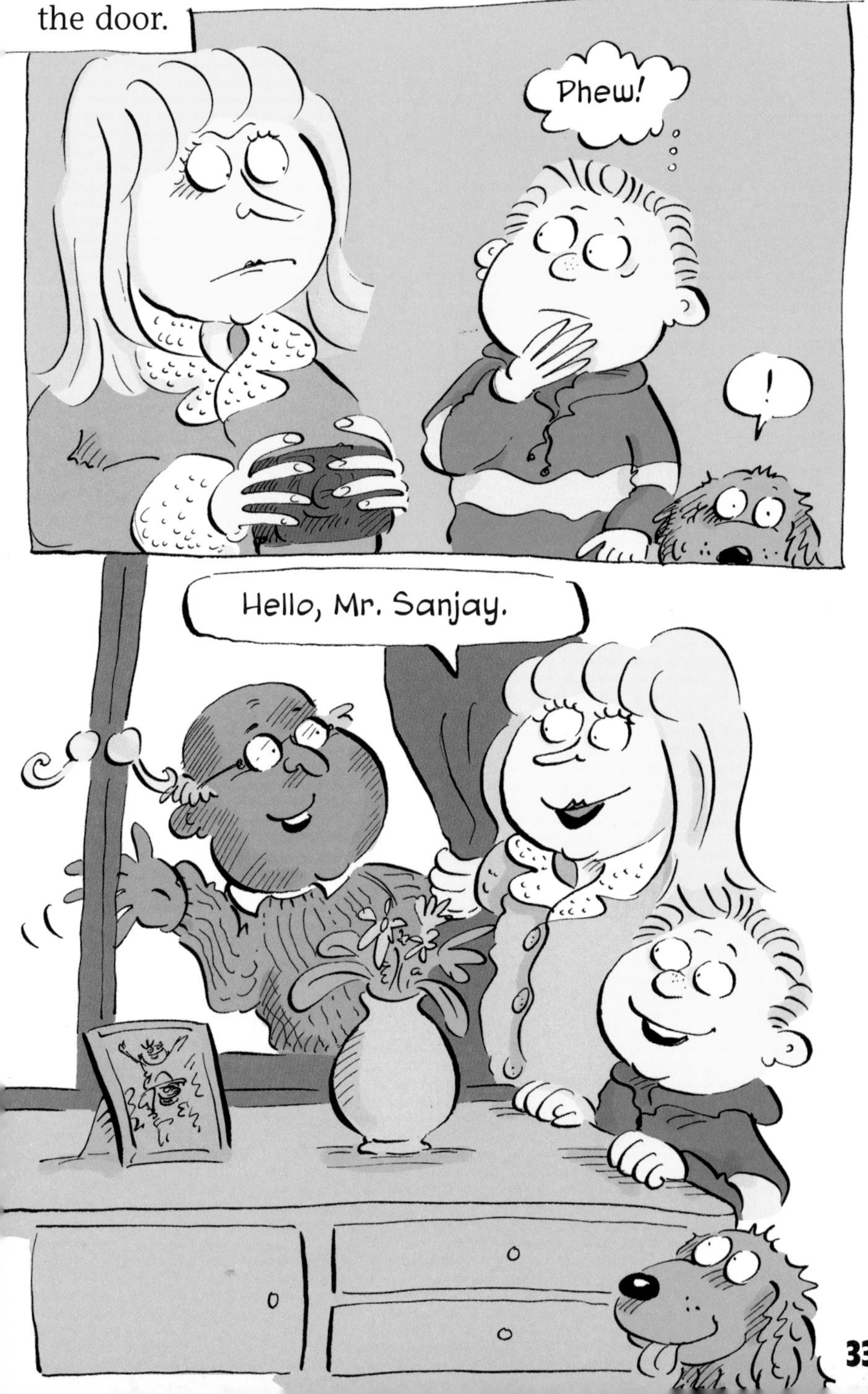
Phew!
!
Hello, Mr. Sanjay.

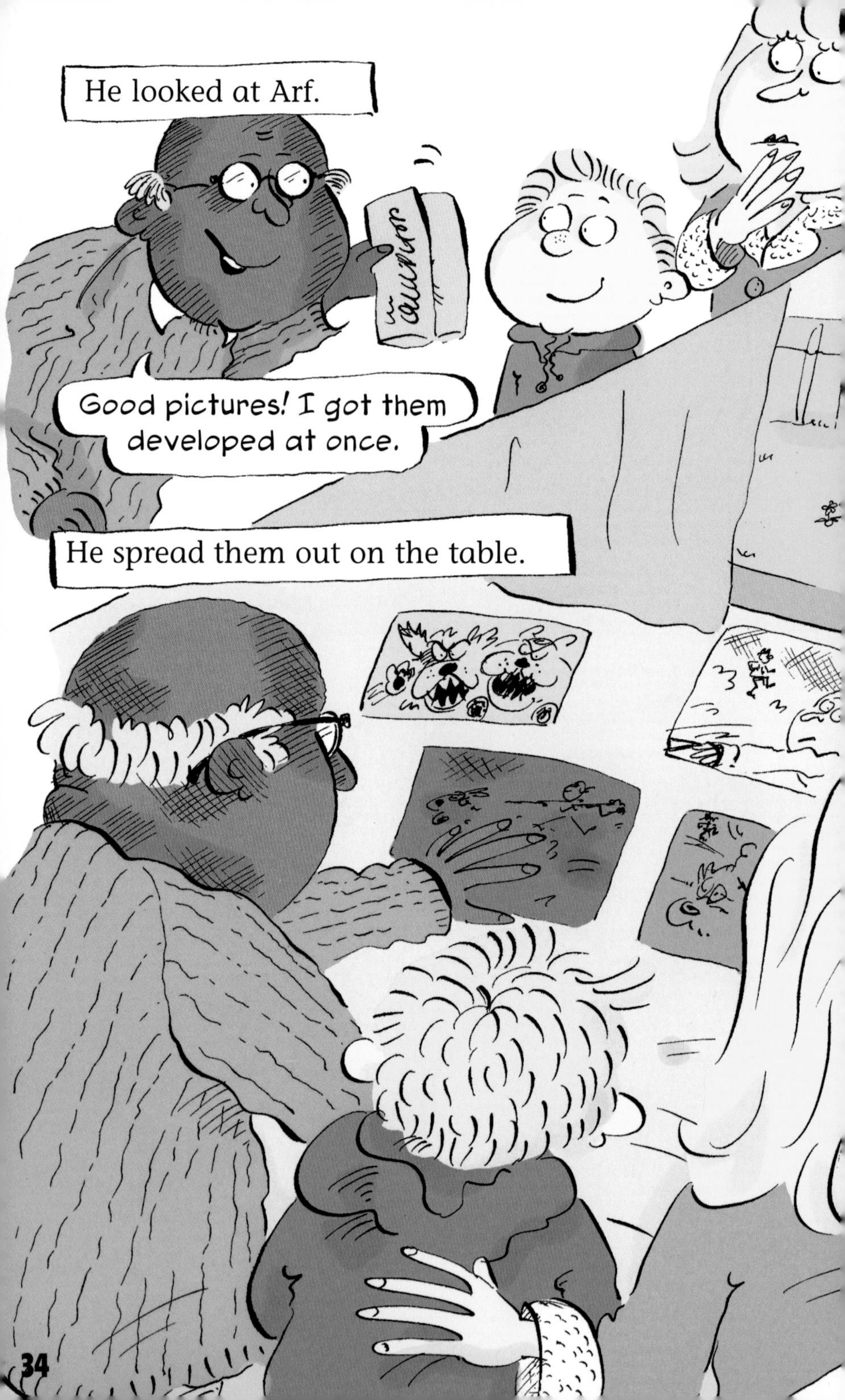
He looked at Arf.
Good pictures! I got them developed at once.
He spread them out on the table.

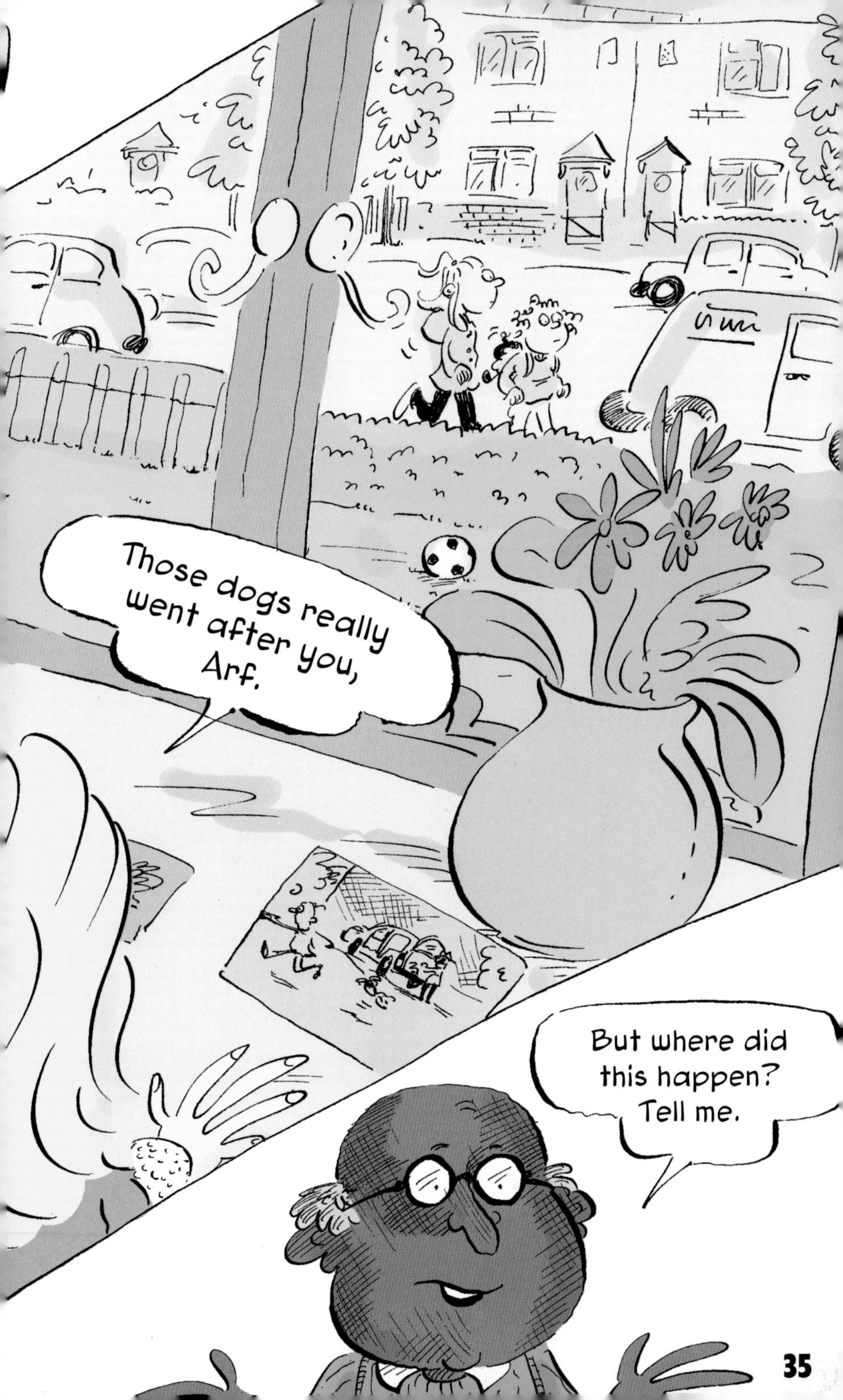
Those dogs really went after you, Arf.
But where did this happen? Tell me.

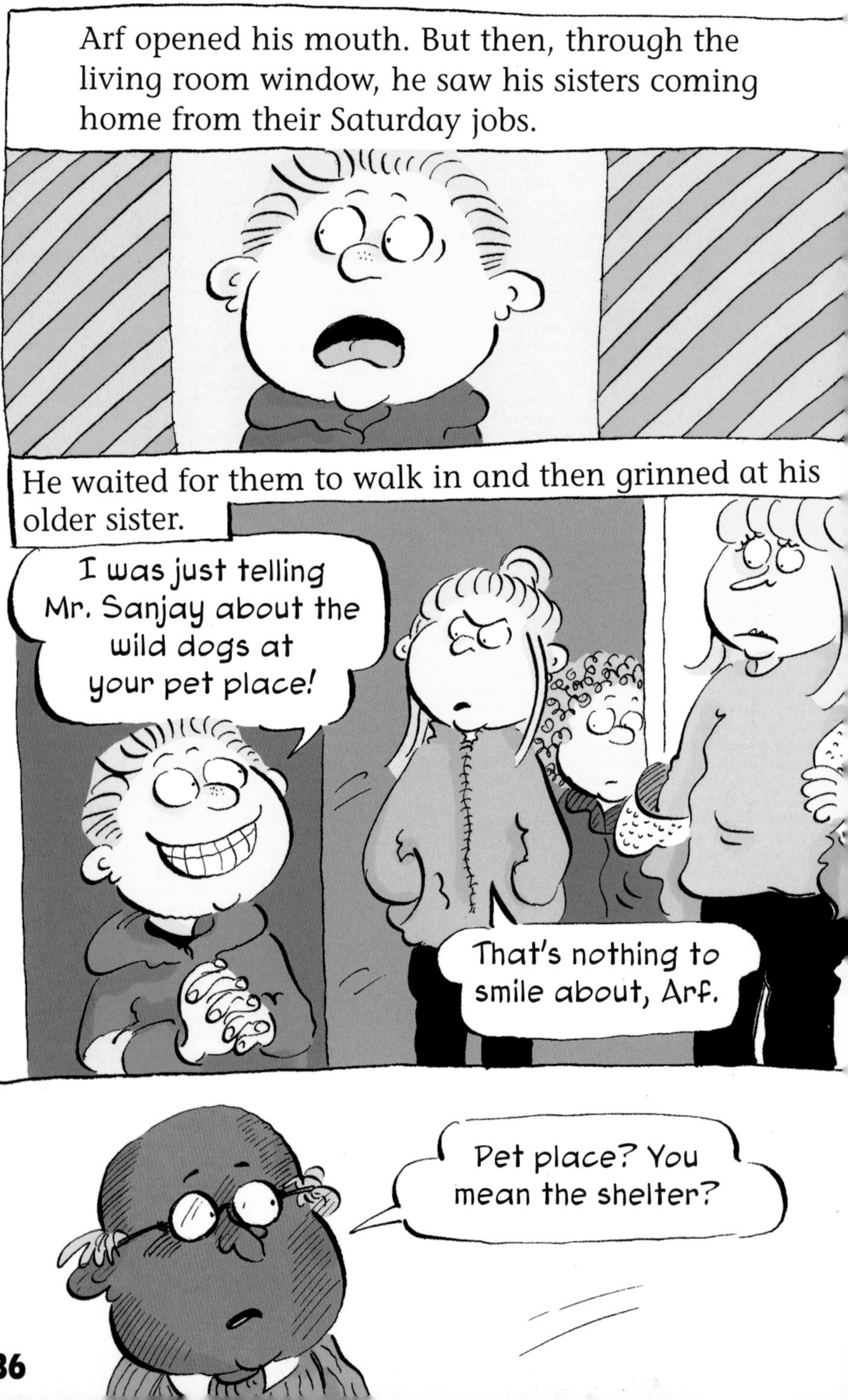
Arf opened his mouth. But then, through the living room window, he saw his sisters coming home from their Saturday jobs.
He waited for them to walk in and then grinned at his older sister.
I was just telling Mr. Sanjay about the wild dogs at your pet place!
That's nothing to smile about, Arf.
Pet place? You mean the shelter?

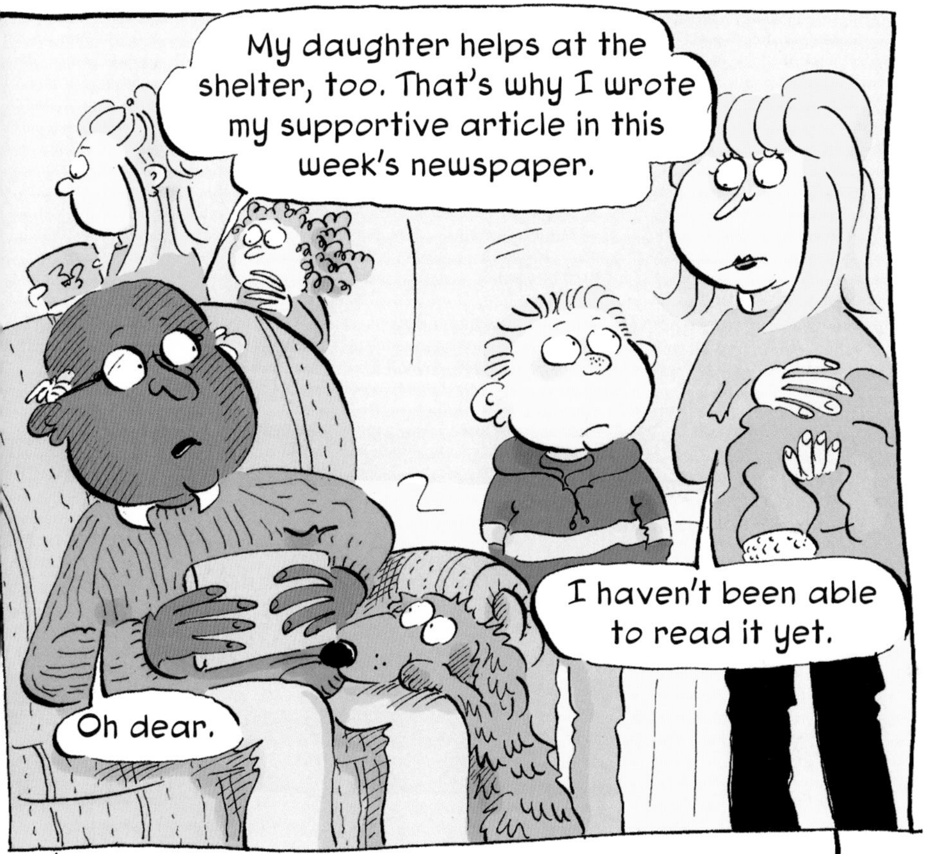
My daughter helps at the shelter, too. That's why I wrote my supportive article in this week's newspaper.
I haven't been able to read it yet.
Oh dear.

Mr. Sanjay explained why he wrote the article.

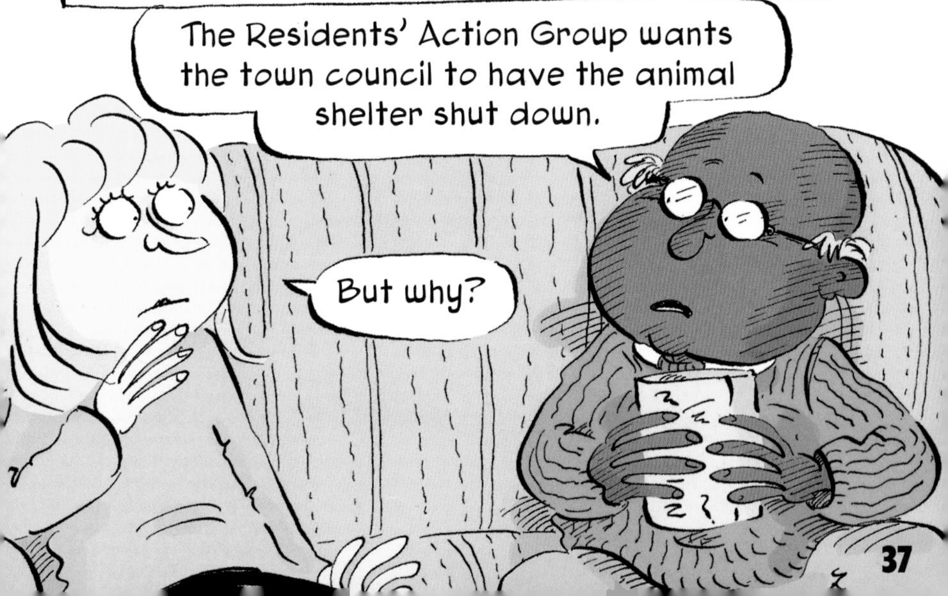
The Residents' Action Group wants the town council to have the animal shelter shut down.
But why?

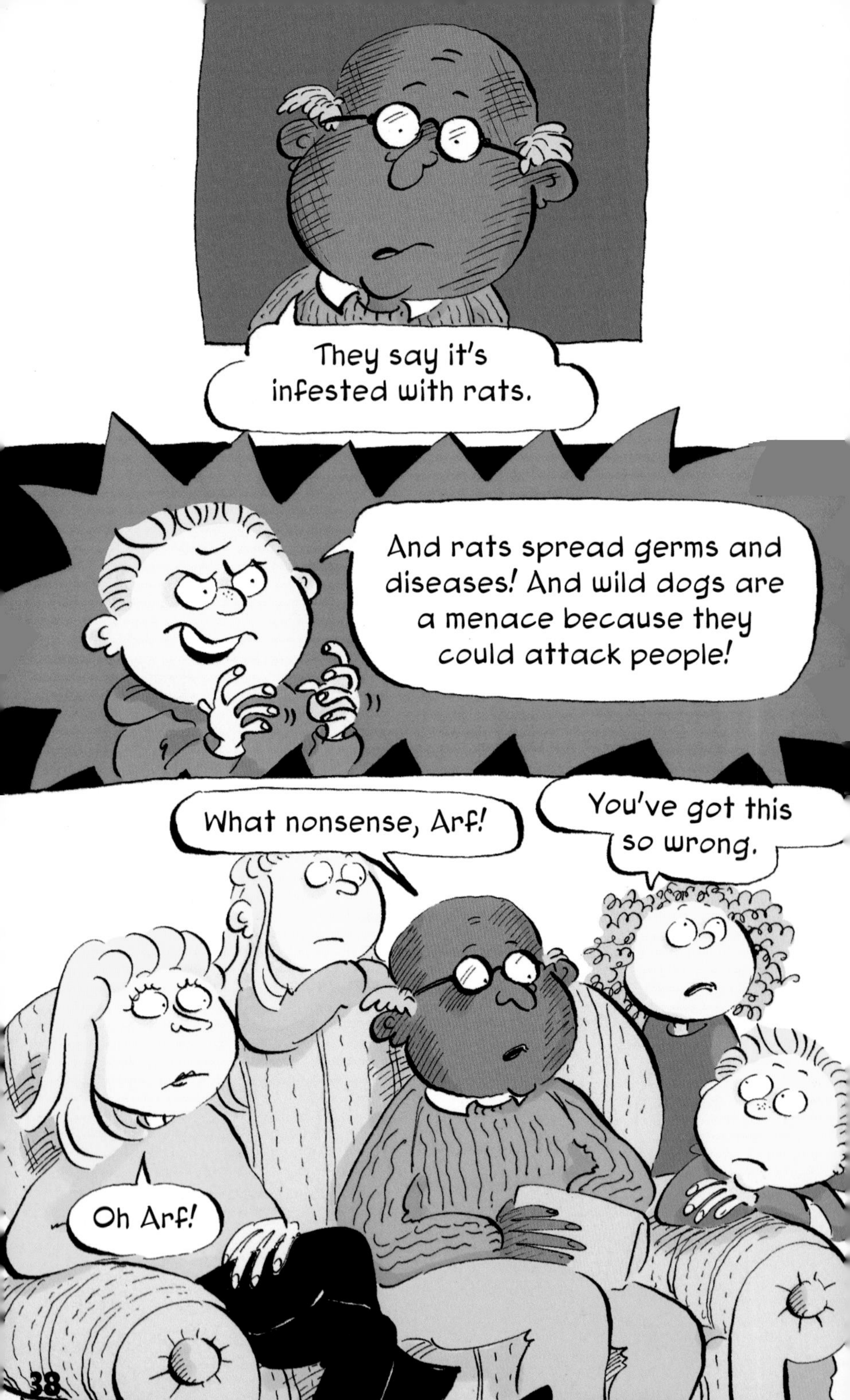
They say it's infested with rats.
And rats spread germs and diseases! And wild dogs are a menace because they could attack people!
What nonsense, Arf!
You've got this so wrong.
Oh Arf!

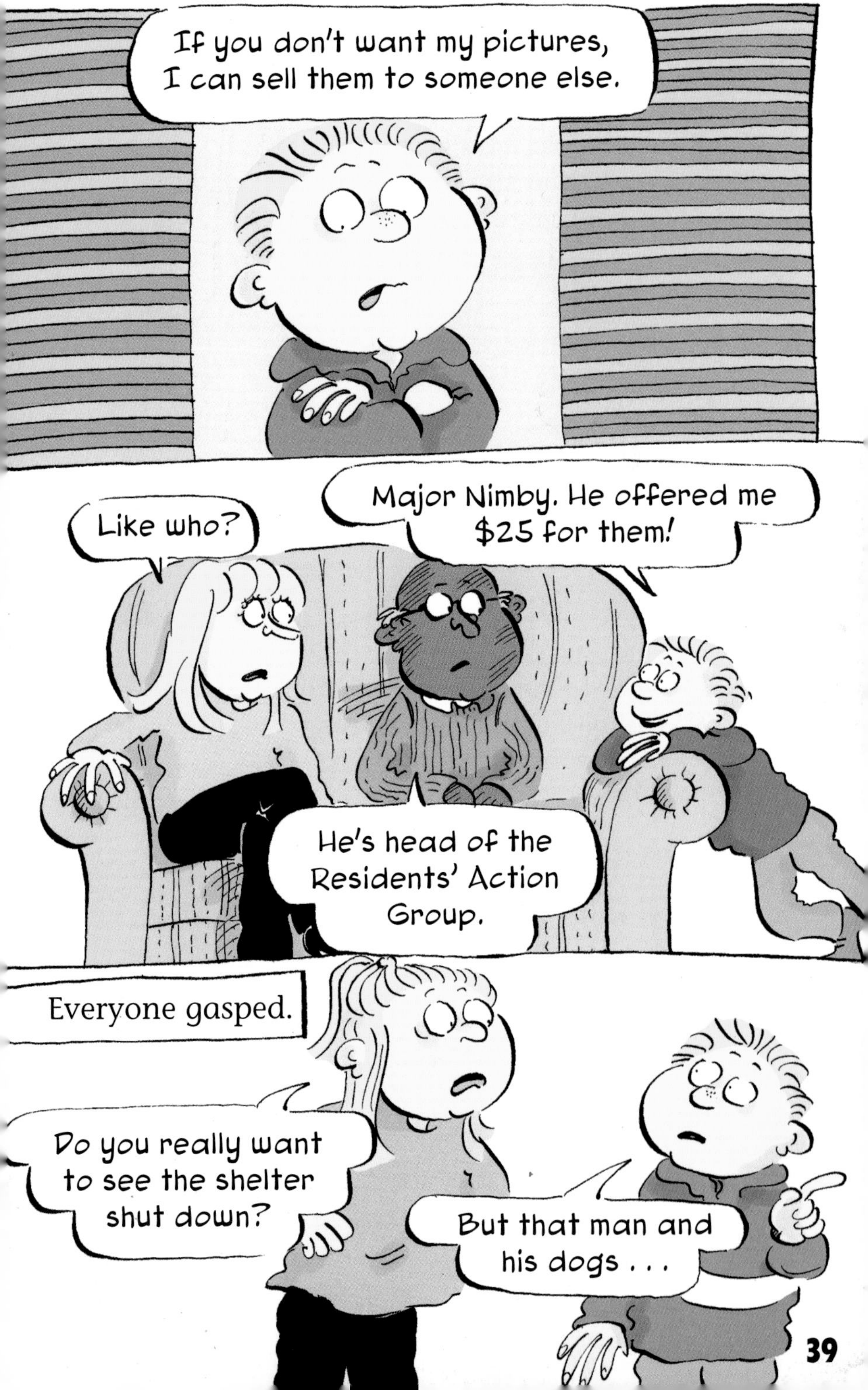
If you don't want my pictures, I can sell them to someone else.
Like who?
Major Nimby. He offered me $25 for them!
He's head of the Residents' Action Group.
Everyone gasped.
Do you really want to see the shelter shut down?
But that man and his dogs . . .

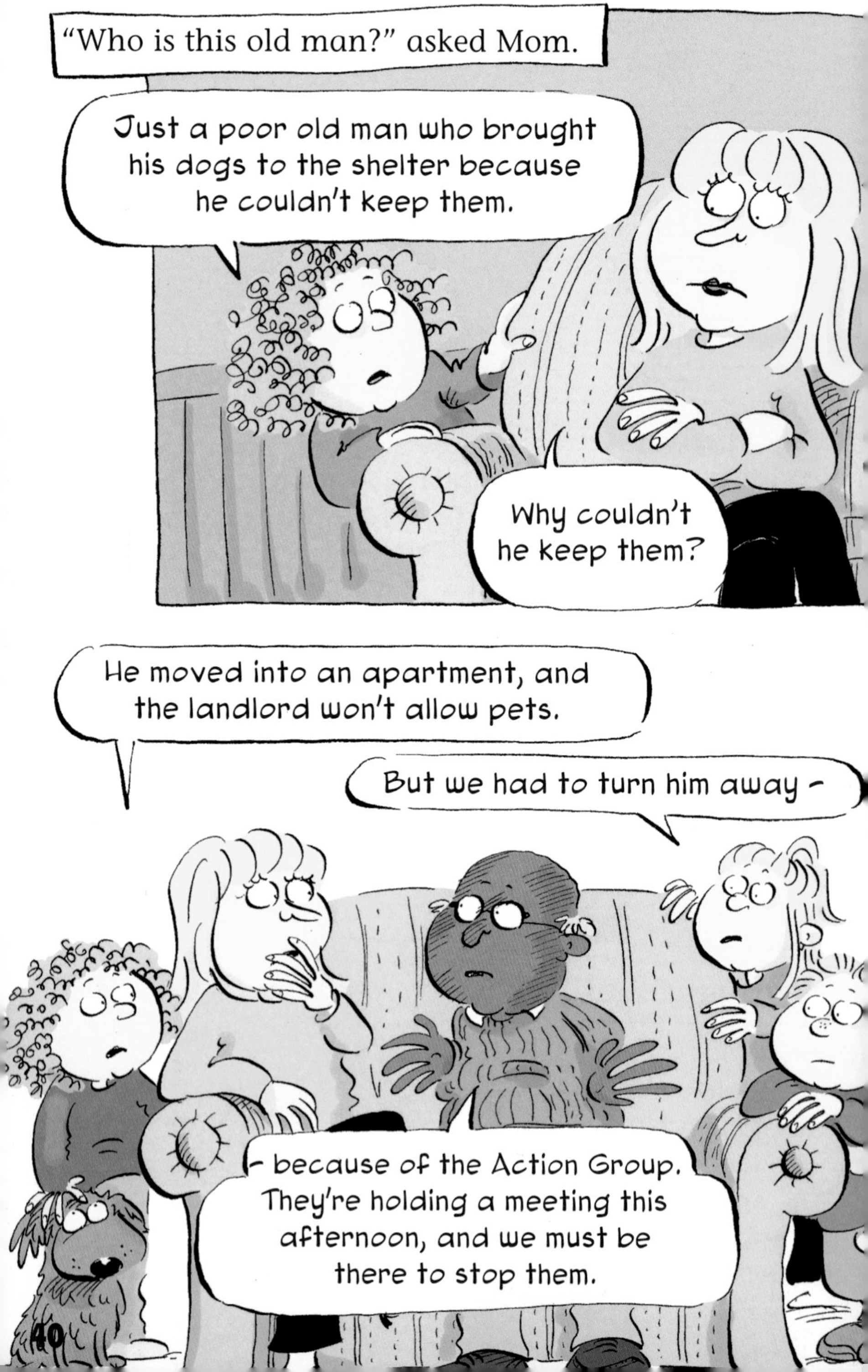
"Who is this old man?" asked Mom.
Just a poor old man who brought his dogs to the shelter because he couldn't keep them.
Why couldn't he keep them?
He moved into an apartment, and the landlord won't allow pets.
But we had to turn him away -
- because of the Action Group. They're holding a meeting this afternoon, and we must be there to stop them.

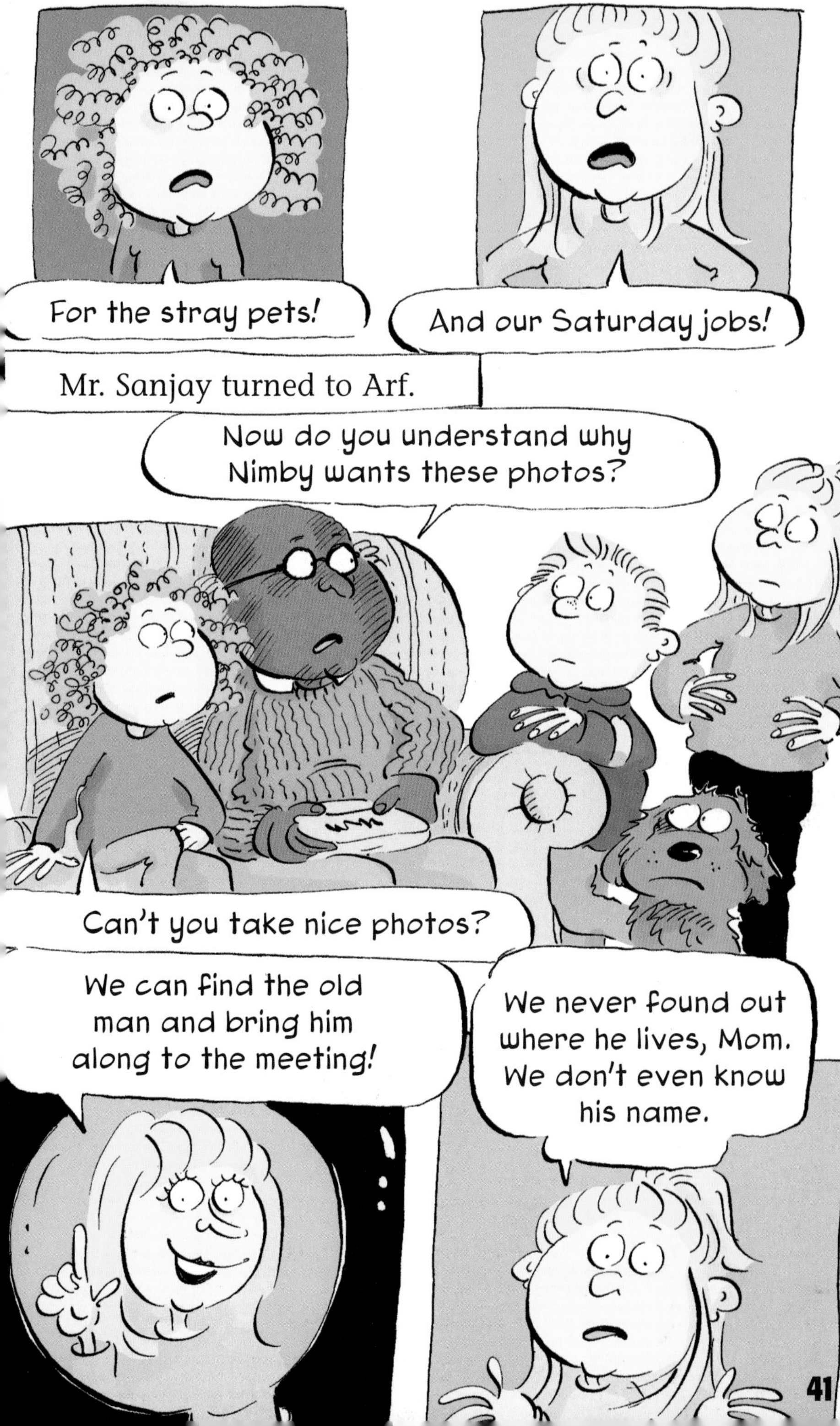
For the stray pets!
And our Saturday jobs!
Mr. Sanjay turned to Arf.
Now do you understand why Nimby wants these photos?
Can't you take nice photos?
We can find the old man and bring him along to the meeting!
We never found out where he lives, Mom. We don't even know his name.

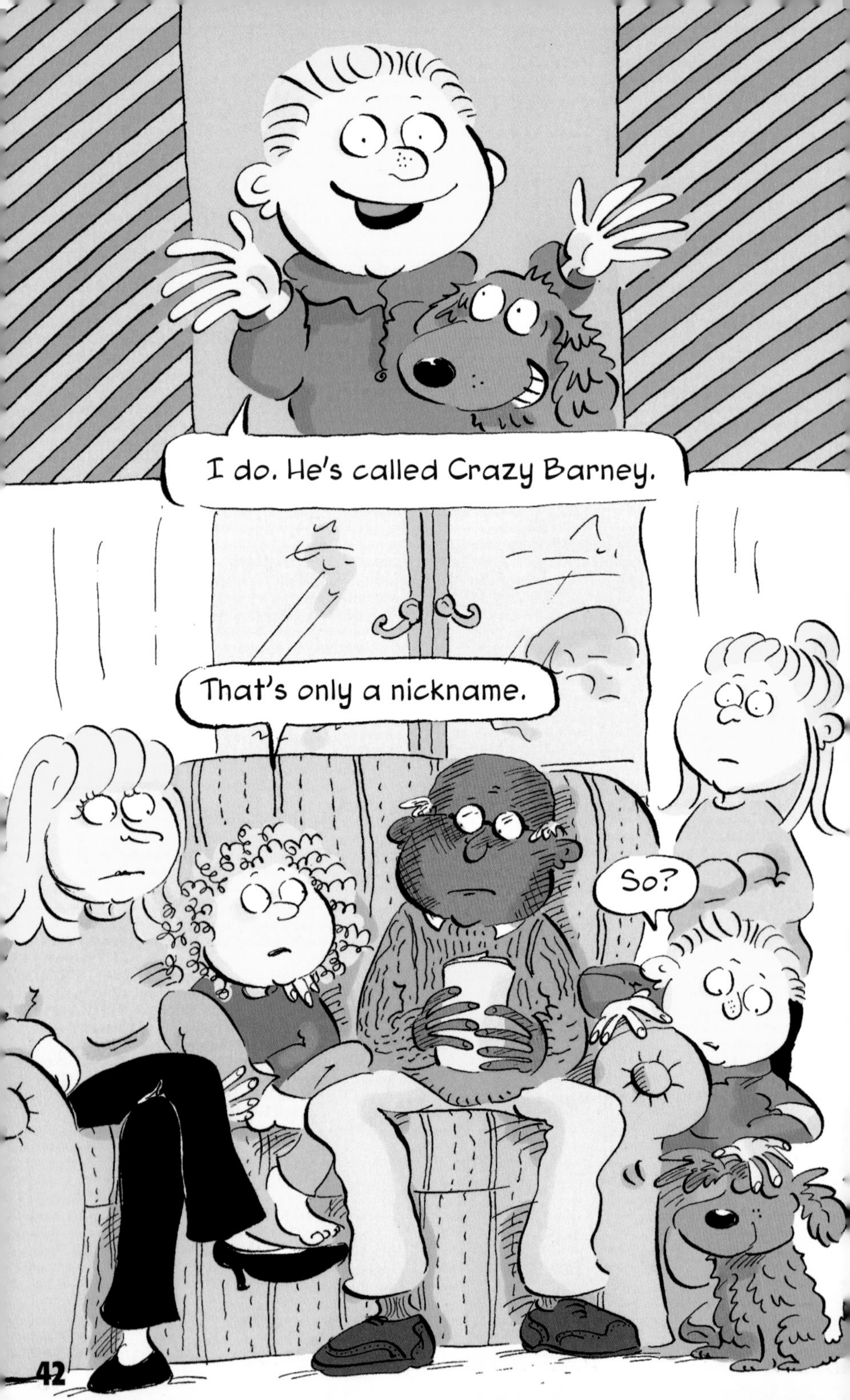
I do. He's called Crazy Barney.
That's only a nickname.
So?

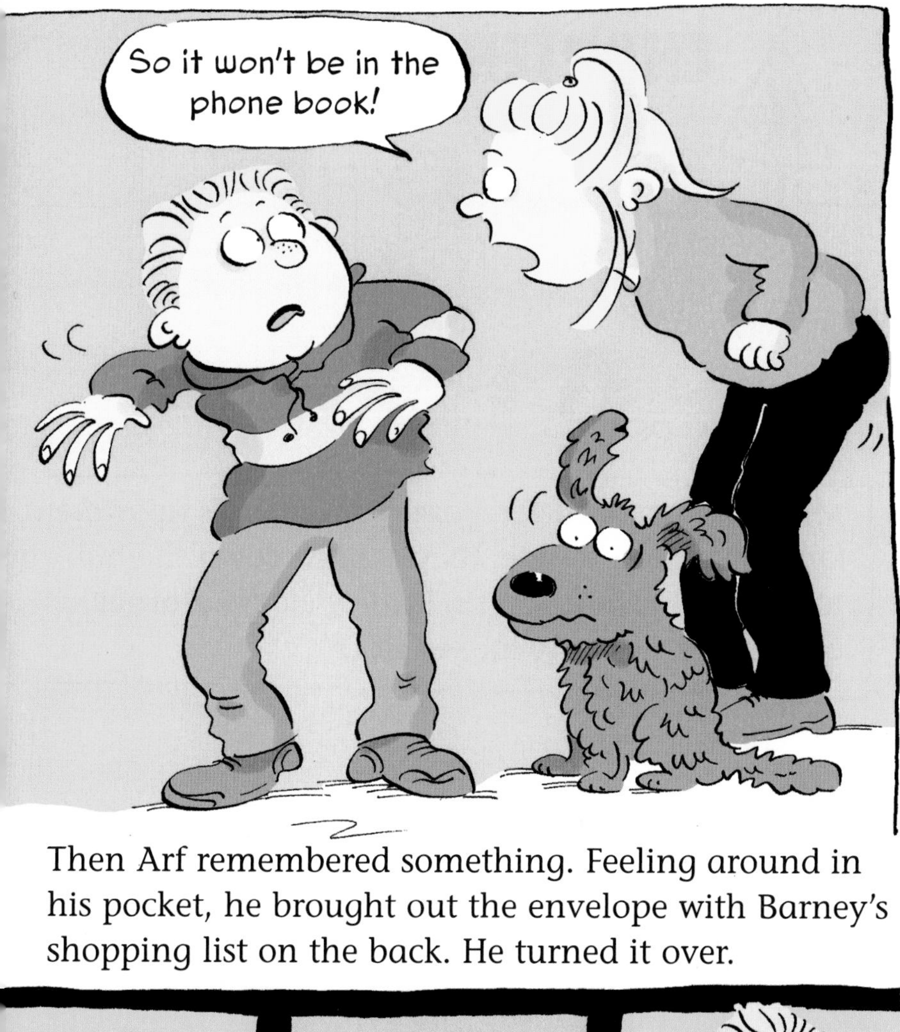
So it won't be in the phone book!

Then Arf remembered something. Feeling around in his pocket, he brought out the envelope with Barney's shopping list on the back. He turned it over.

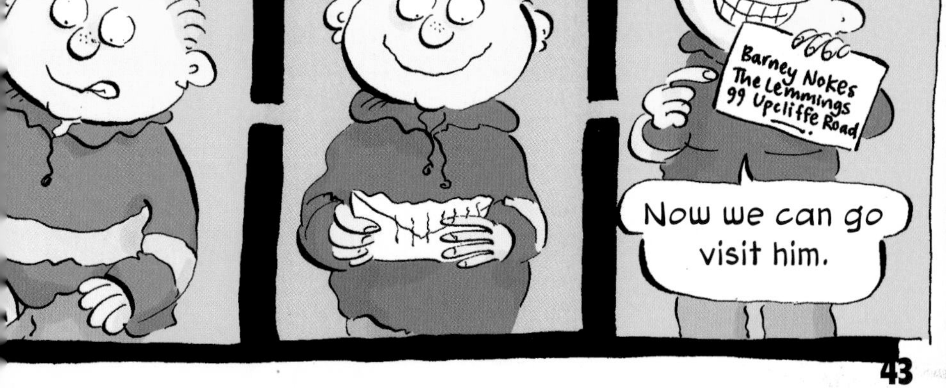
Barney Nokes
The Lemmings
99 Upcliffe Road
Now we can go visit him.

CHAPTER FIVE

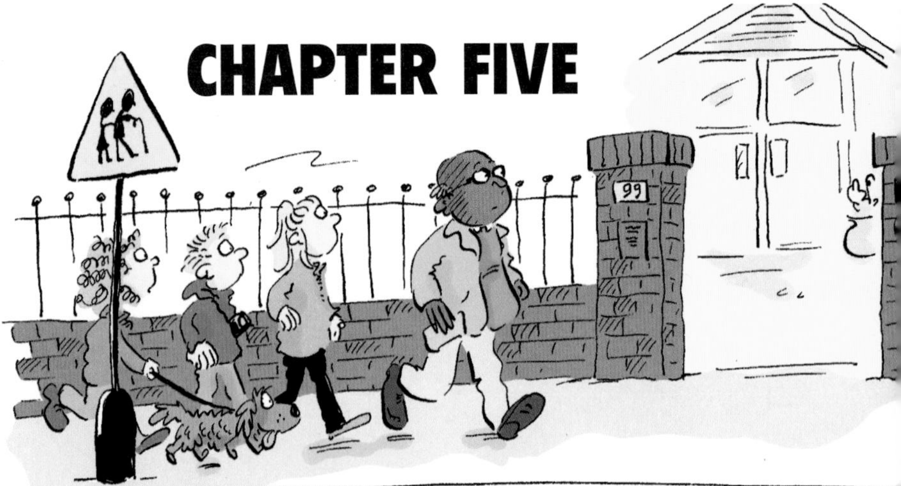
99

Mr. Sanjay pressed the buzzer at Barney's apartment. Once they were inside, they walked down the hallway to apartment number 12, Barney Nokes. Barney opened the door. He looked sad.

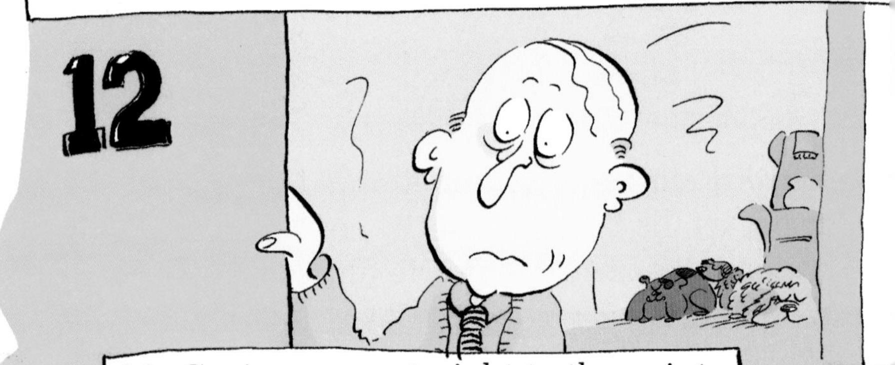
12

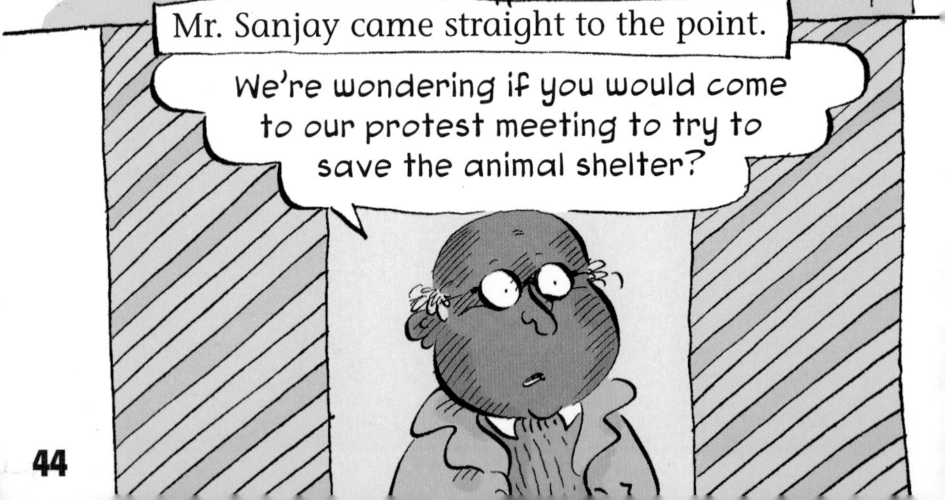
Mr. Sanjay came straight to the point.
We're wondering if you would come to our protest meeting to try to save the animal shelter?

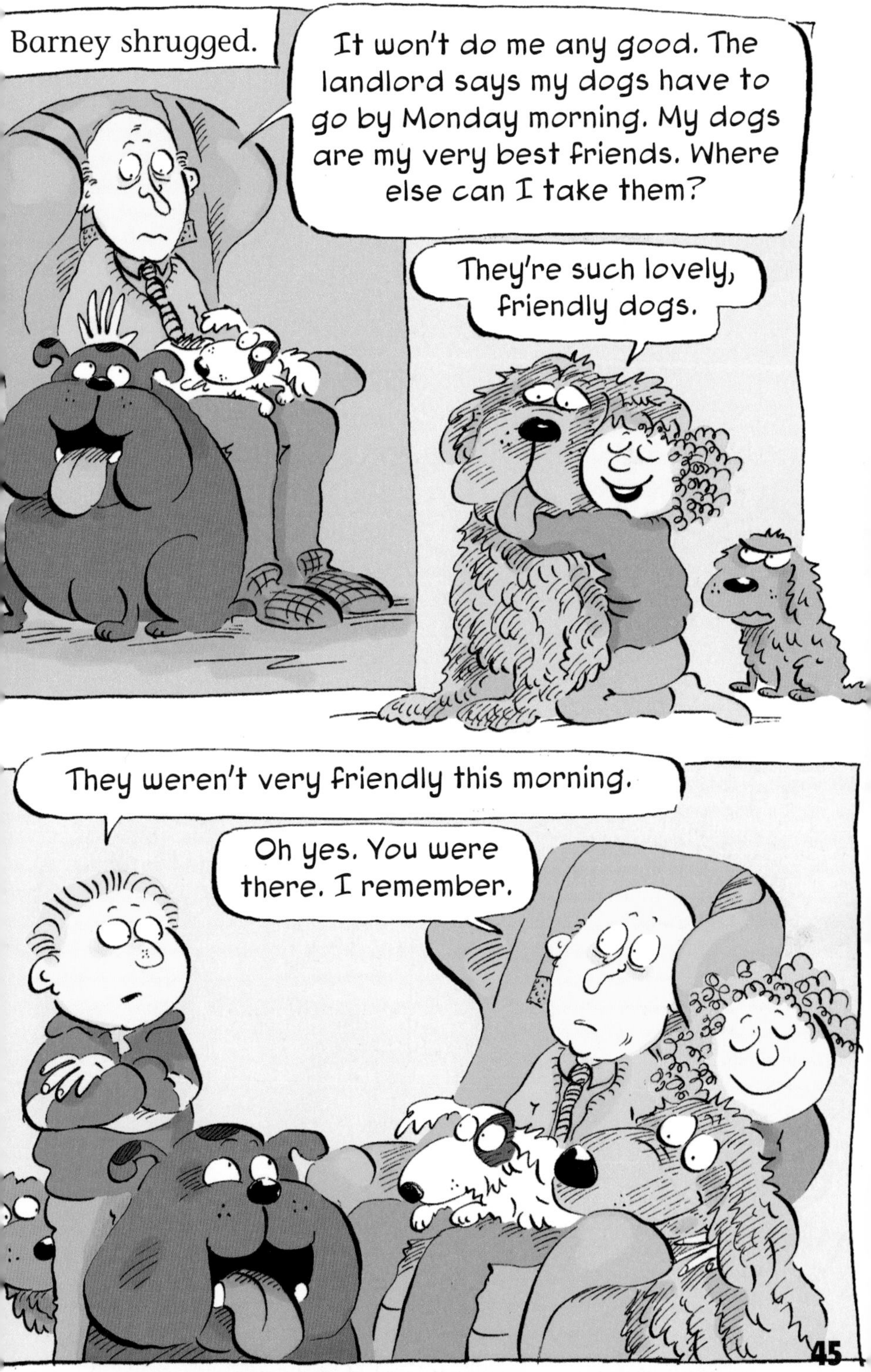
Barney shrugged.
It won't do me any good. The landlord says my dogs have to go by Monday morning. My dogs are my very best friends. Where else can I take them?
They're such lovely, friendly dogs.
They weren't very friendly this morning.
Oh yes. You were there. I remember.

Arf looked through his photos, only to drop the envelope containing the lottery ticket.

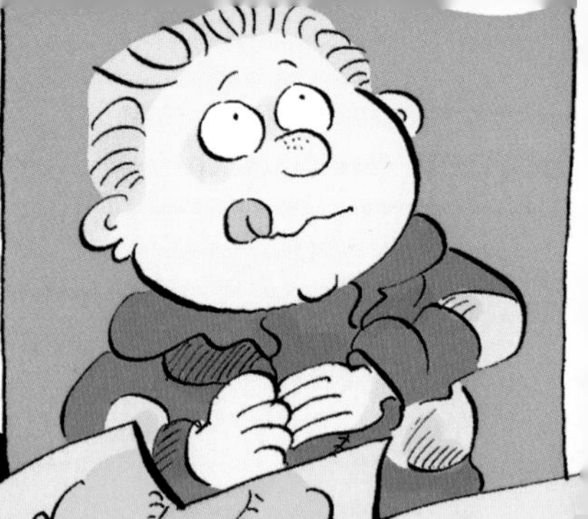

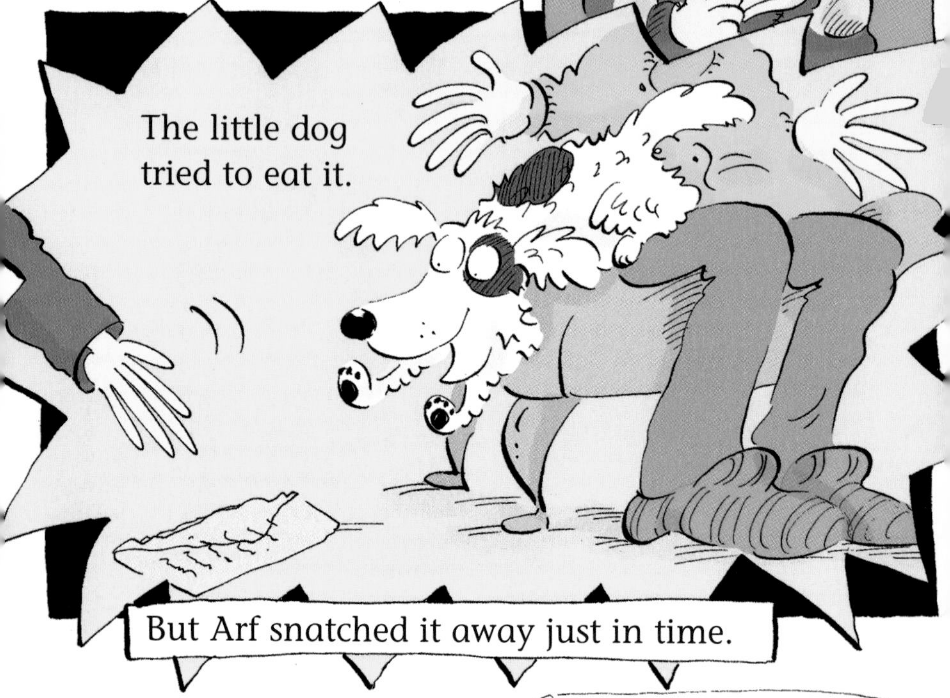

The little dog tried to eat it.

But Arf snatched it away just in time.

He put it down on the table, next to the newspaper, and then he showed Barney the pictures.

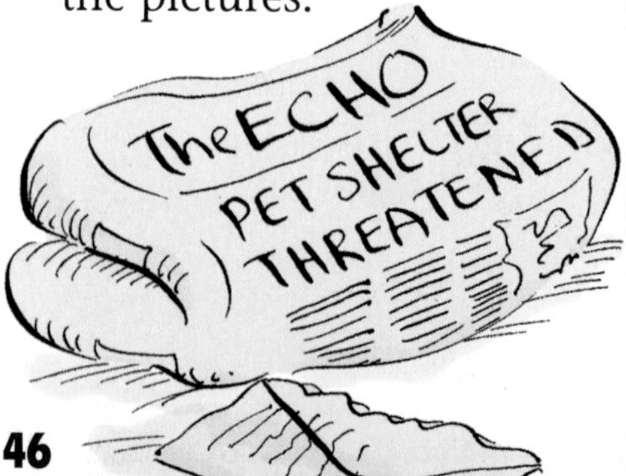
The ECHO
PET SHELTER THREATENED

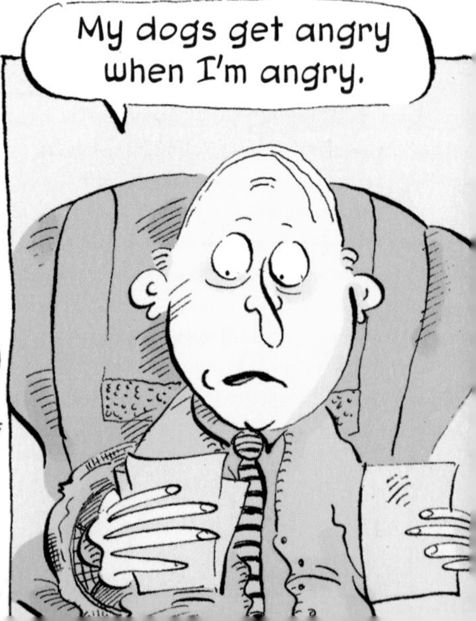
My dogs get angry when I'm angry.

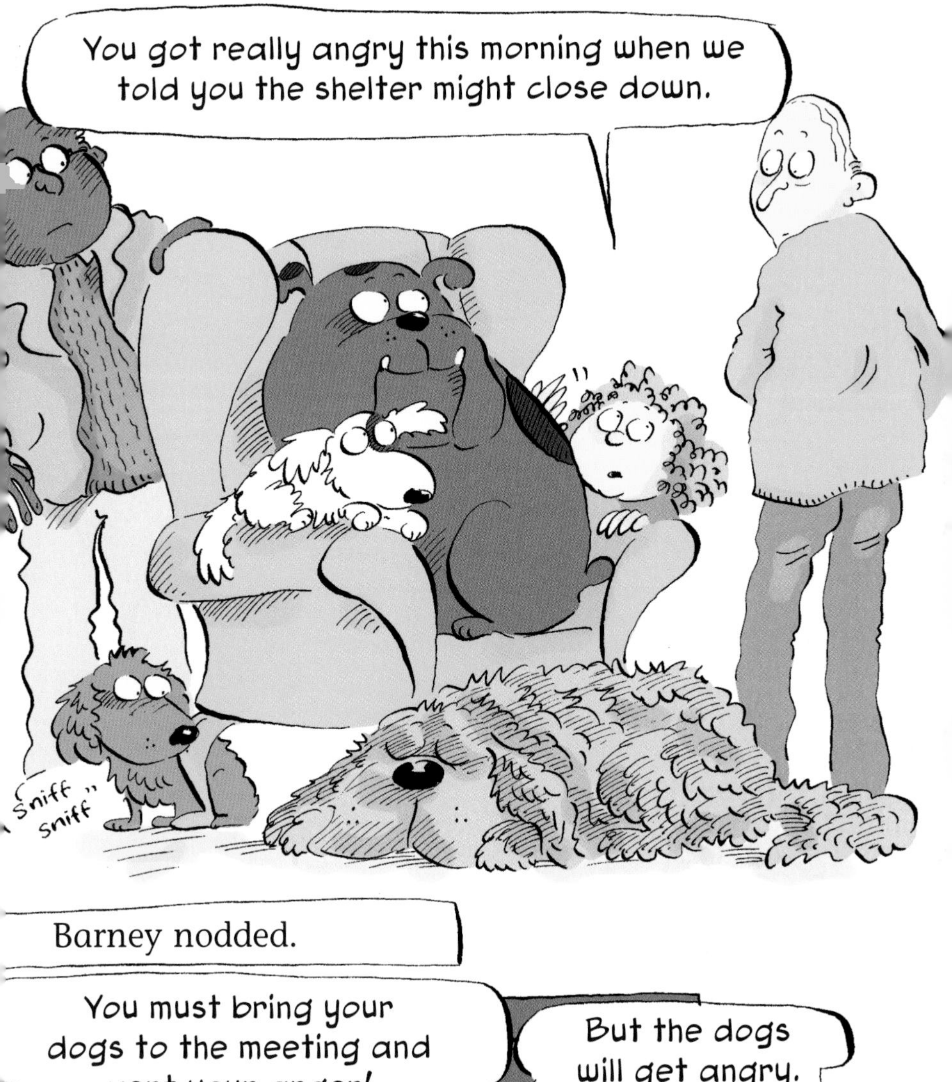
You got really angry this morning when we told you the shelter might close down.
sniff sniff

Barney nodded.

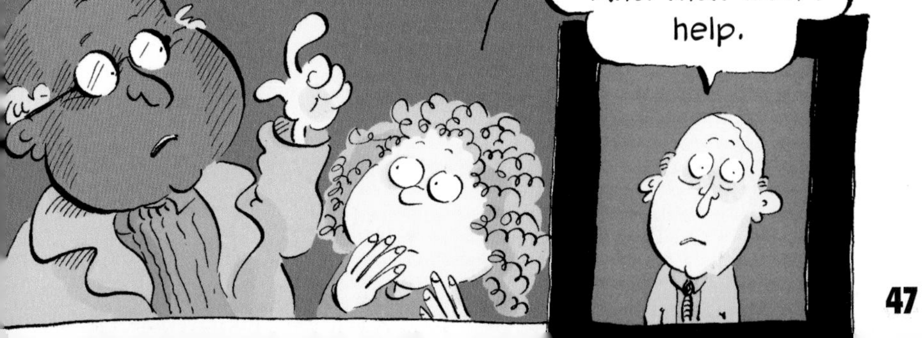
You must bring your dogs to the meeting and vent your anger!
But the dogs will get angry.
And that won't help.

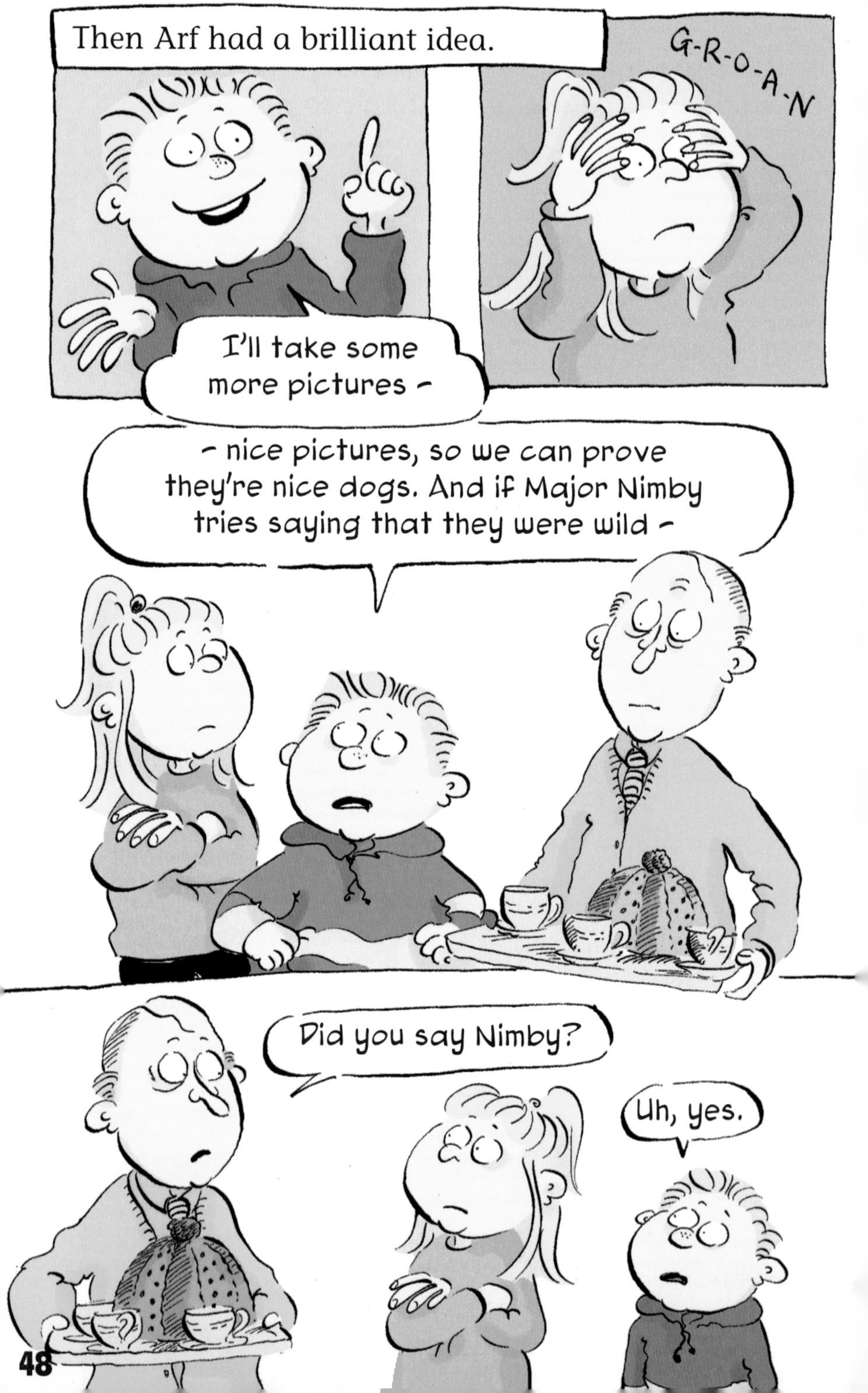
Then Arf had a brilliant idea.
G-R-O-A-N
I'll take some more pictures –
– nice pictures, so we can prove they're nice dogs. And if Major Nimby tries saying that they were wild –
Did you say Nimby?
Uh, yes.

Now Barney looked really angry.

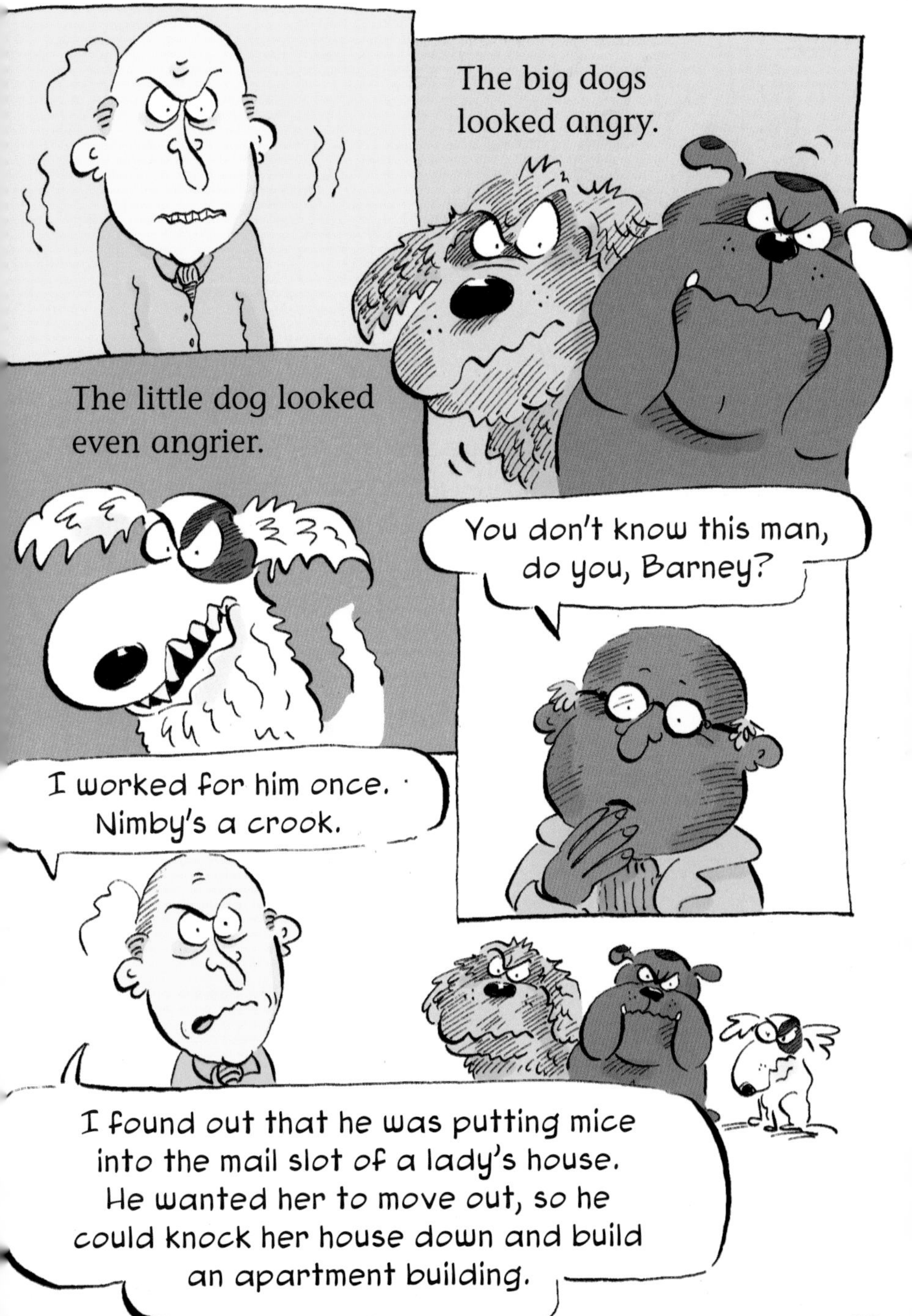
The big dogs looked angry.
The little dog looked even angrier.
You don't know this man, do you, Barney?
I worked for him once. Nimby's a crook.
I found out that he was putting mice into the mail slot of a lady's house. He wanted her to move out, so he could knock her house down and build an apartment building.

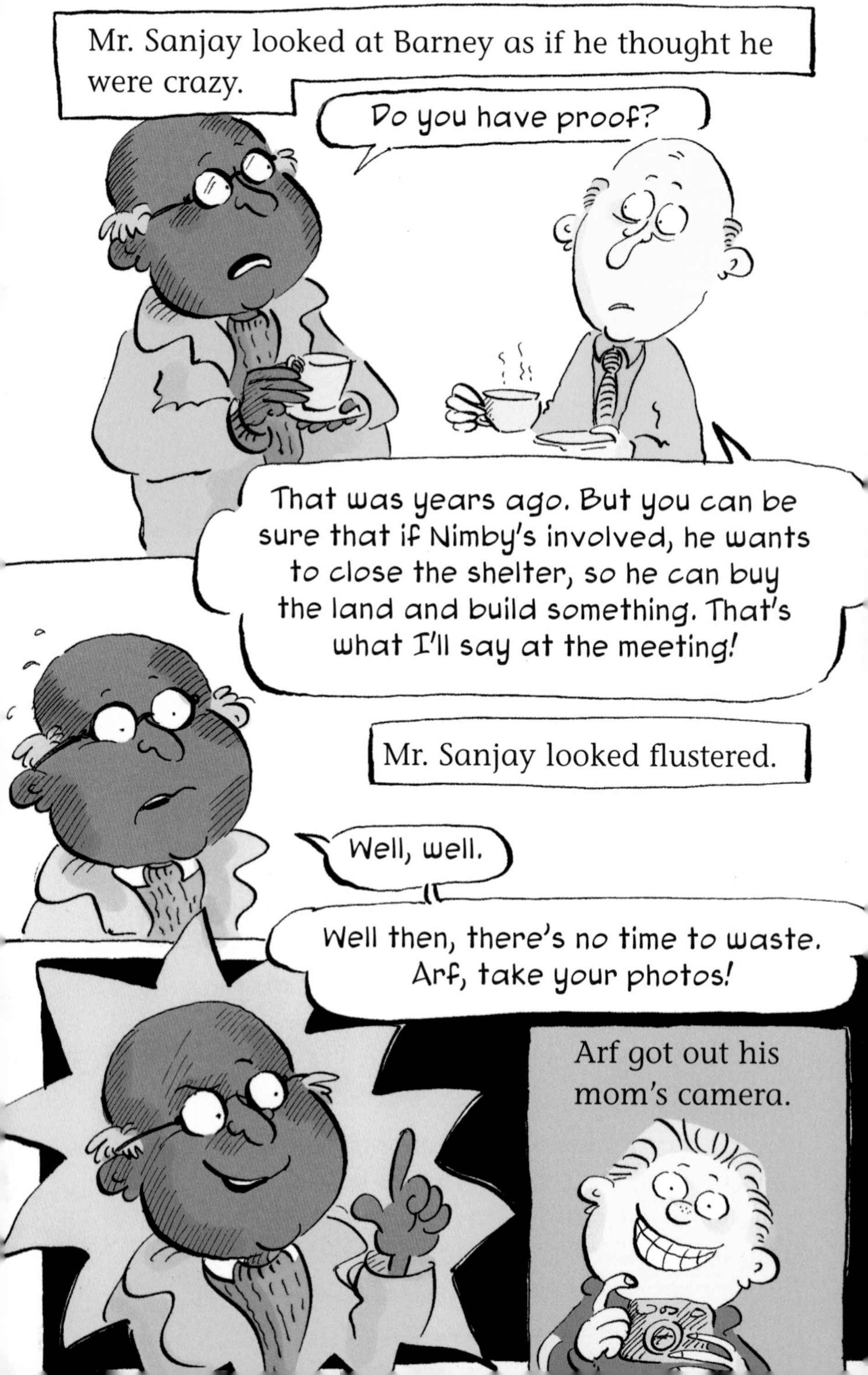

Mr. Sanjay looked at Barney as if he thought he were crazy.
Do you have proof?
That was years ago. But you can be sure that if Nimby's involved, he wants to close the shelter, so he can buy the land and build something. That's what I'll say at the meeting!
Mr. Sanjay looked flustered.
Well, well.
Well then, there's no time to waste. Arf, take your photos!
Arf got out his mom's camera.

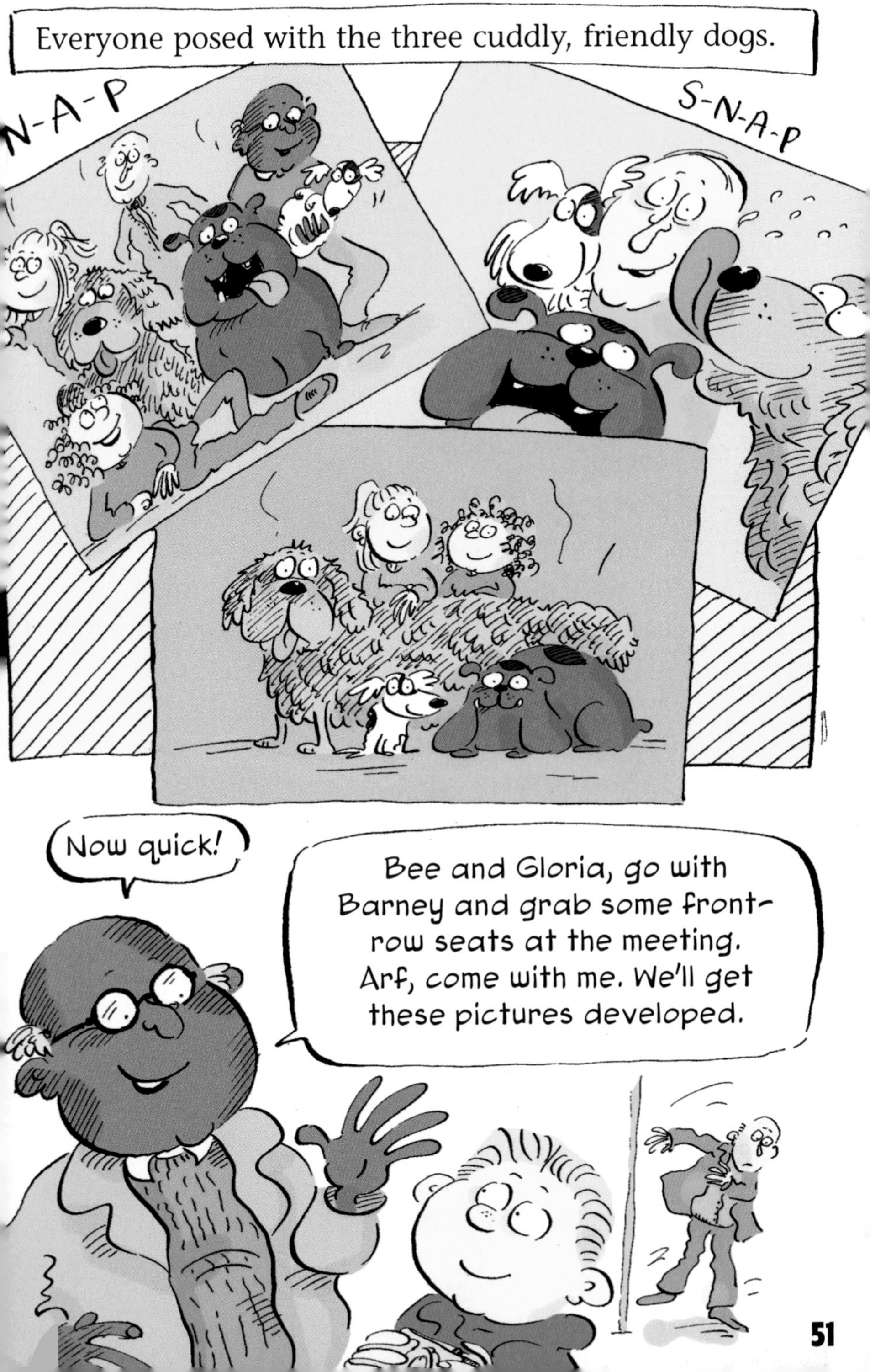
Everyone posed with the three cuddly, friendly dogs.
N-A-P
S-N-A-P
Now quick!
Bee and Gloria, go with Barney and grab some front-row seats at the meeting. Arf, come with me. We'll get these pictures developed.

CHAPTER SIX

It took longer to develop Arf's film than Mr. Sanjay expected. There was lots of traffic, too.

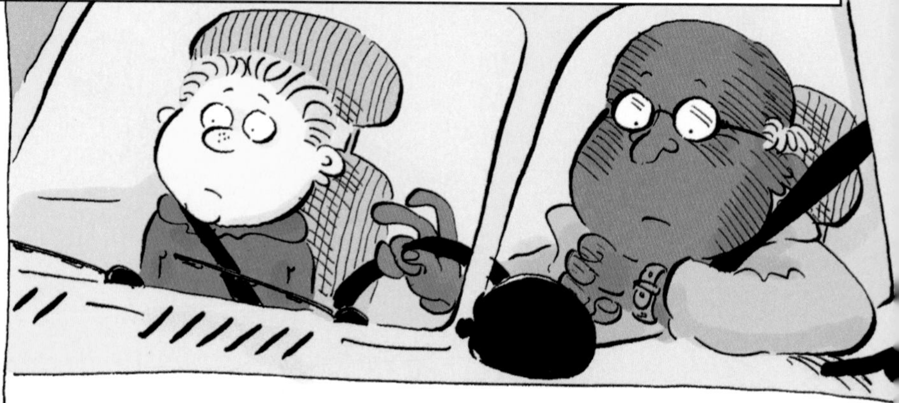

By the time they got to the town hall, the meeting had already started. There were too many people for Arf to see Barney or Bee, or even Gloria, but he could see Major Nimby.

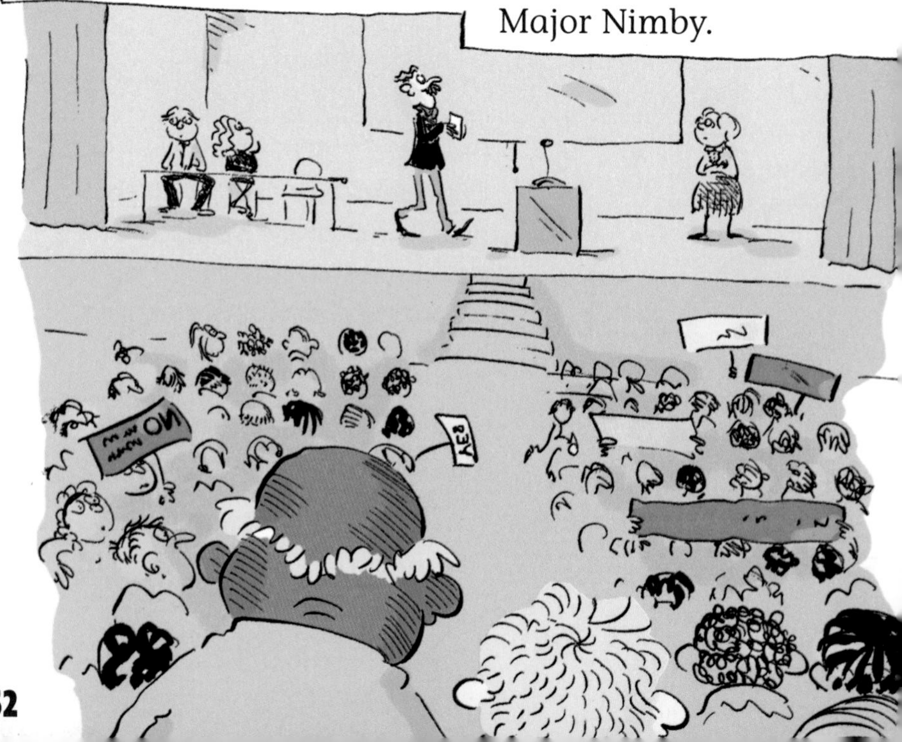

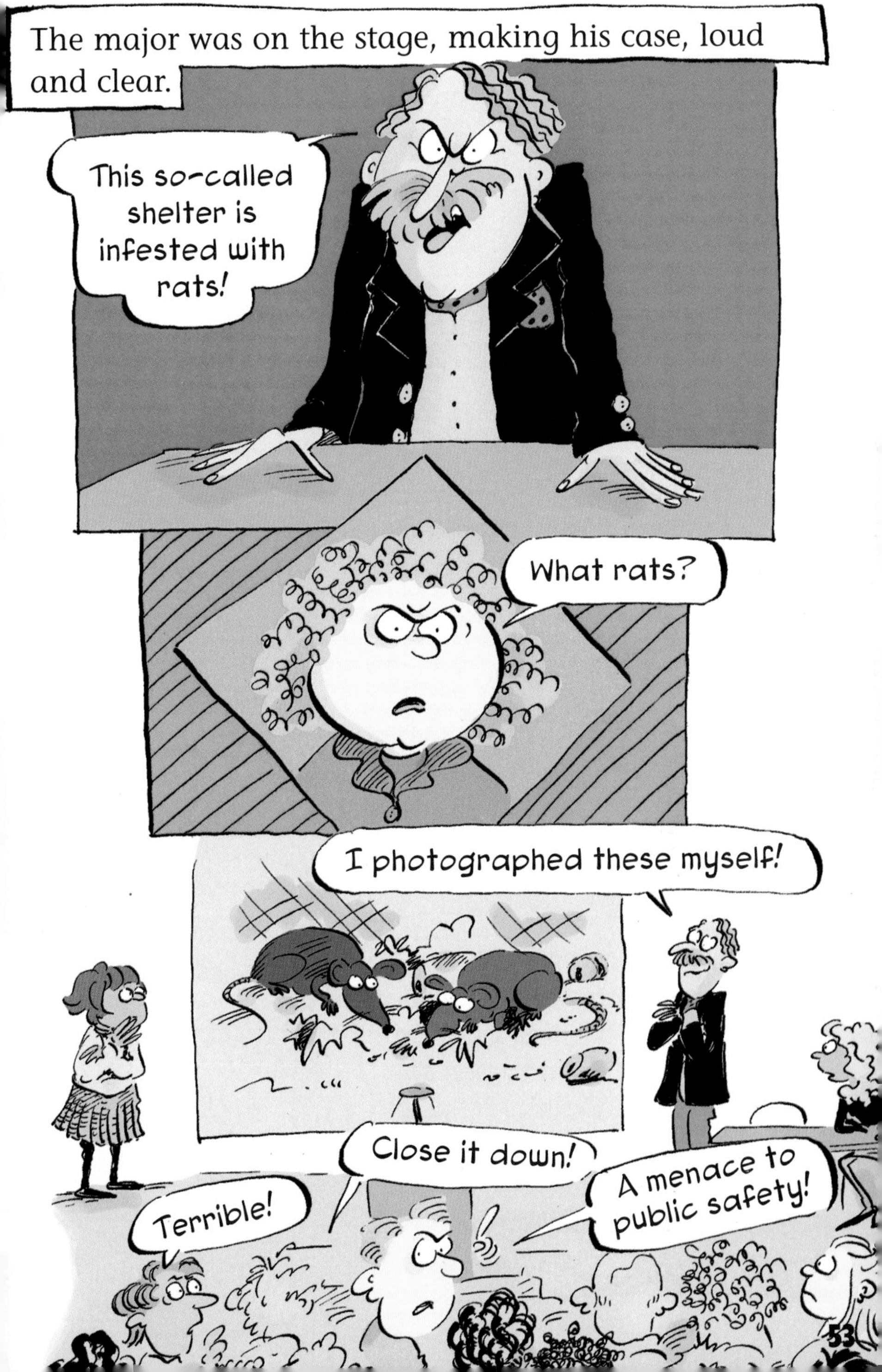
The major was on the stage, making his case, loud and clear.
This so-called shelter is infested with rats!
What rats?
I photographed these myself!
Close it down!
Terrible!
A menace to public safety!

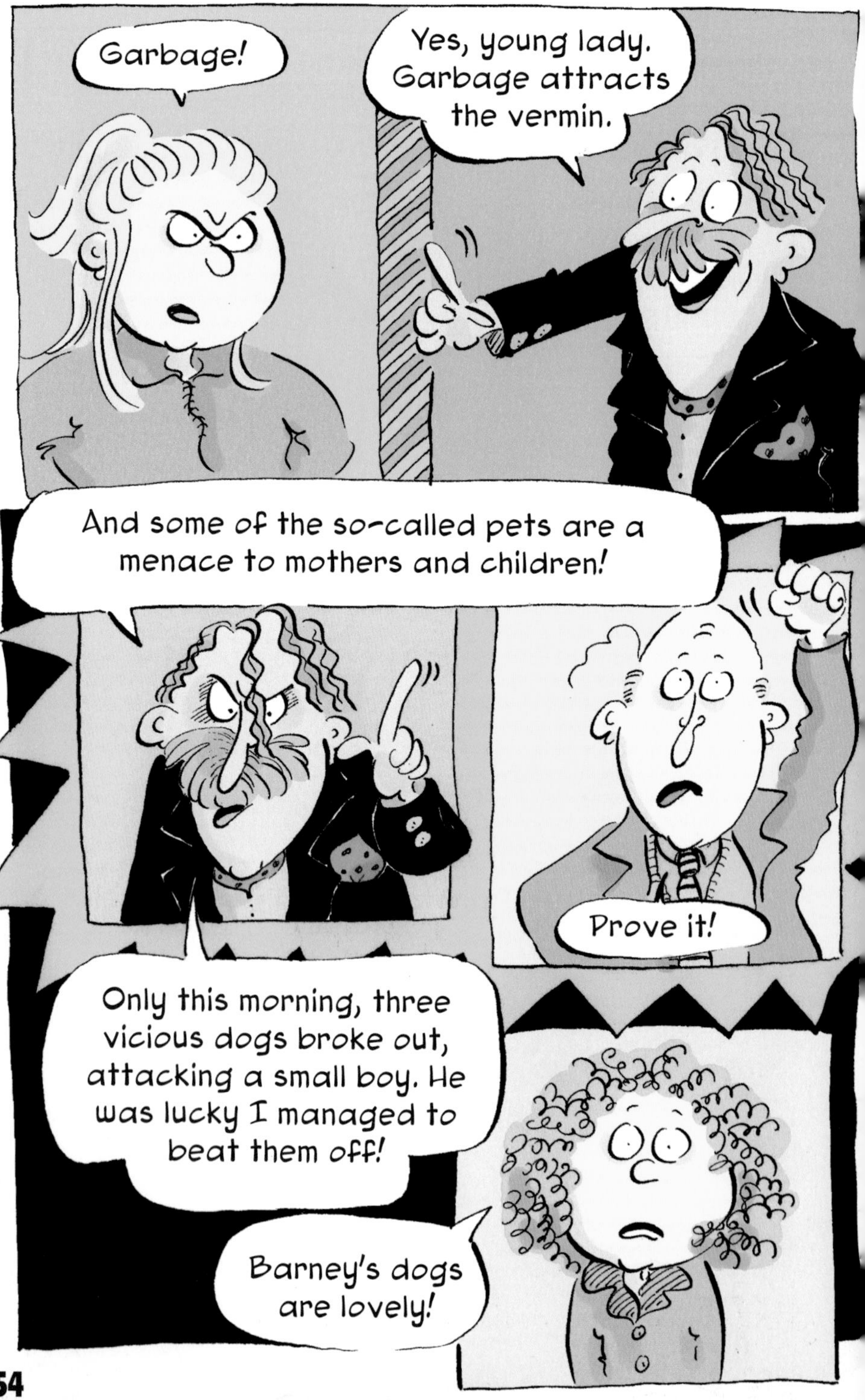
Garbage!
Yes, young lady. Garbage attracts the vermin.
And some of the so-called pets are a menace to mothers and children!
Prove it!
Only this morning, three vicious dogs broke out, attacking a small boy. He was lucky I managed to beat them off!
Barney's dogs are lovely!

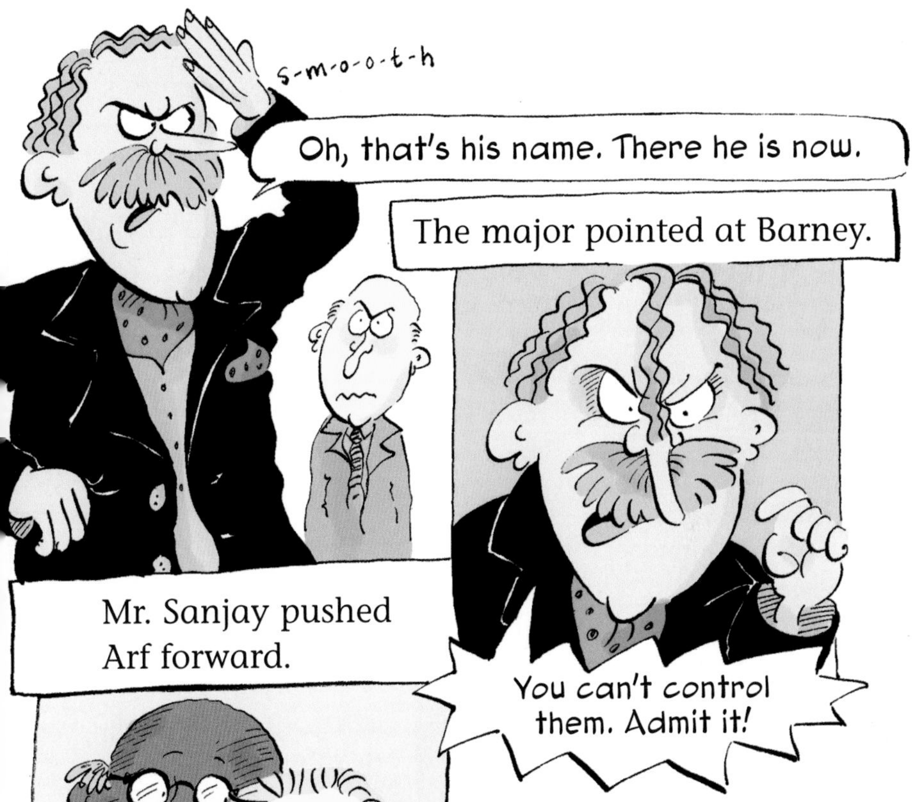
s-m-o-o-t-h
Oh, that's his name. There he is now.
The major pointed at Barney.
You can't control them. Admit it!
Mr. Sanjay pushed Arf forward.

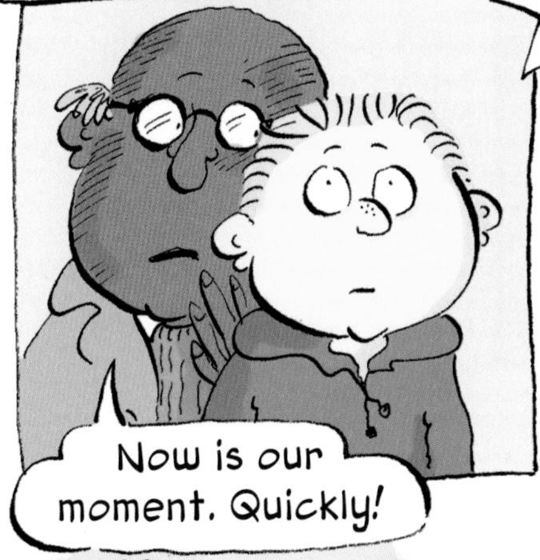
Now is our moment. Quickly!

Arf tried to reach the stage, but people got in the way. He stepped on somebody's toe. This made such a disturbance that Major Nimby noticed.

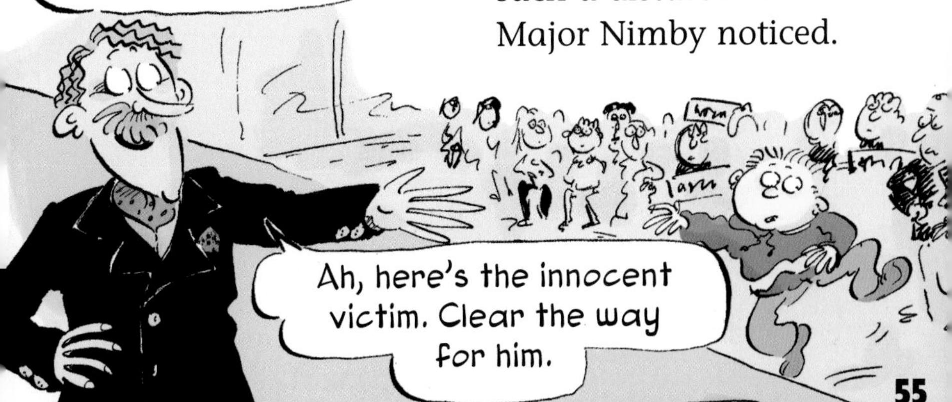
Ah, here's the innocent victim. Clear the way for him.

Arf found himself being lifted by Major Nimby's friends onto the stage beside him.

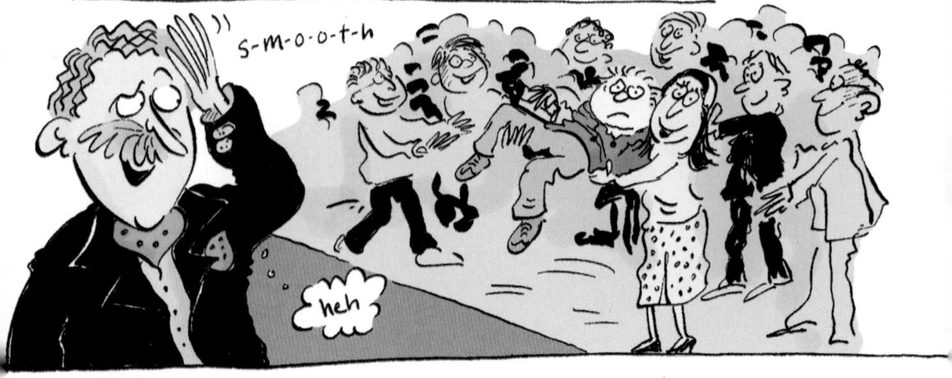
s-m-o-o-t-h
heh

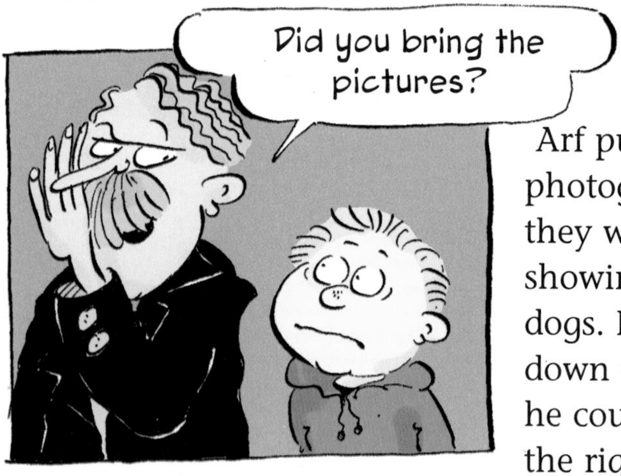
Did you bring the pictures?

Arf pulled out some photographs, but they were the ones showing fierce, angry dogs. He put them down on the table, so he could search for the right ones.

While he was trying to find them, the major grabbed the first photos and gave them to his assistant.

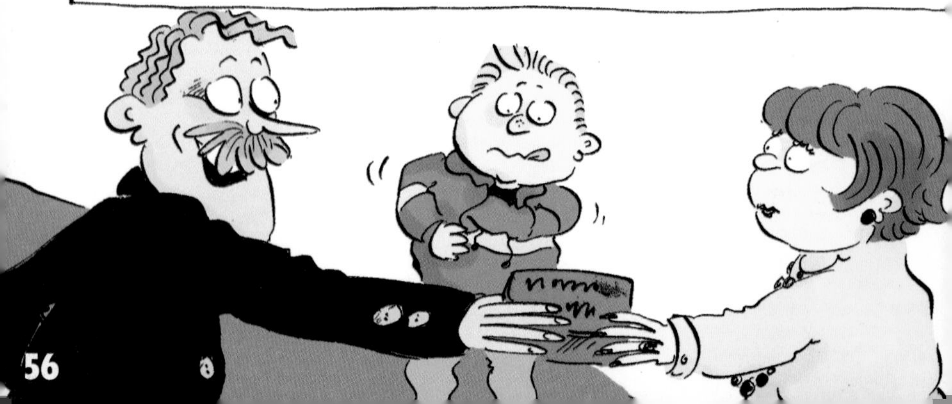

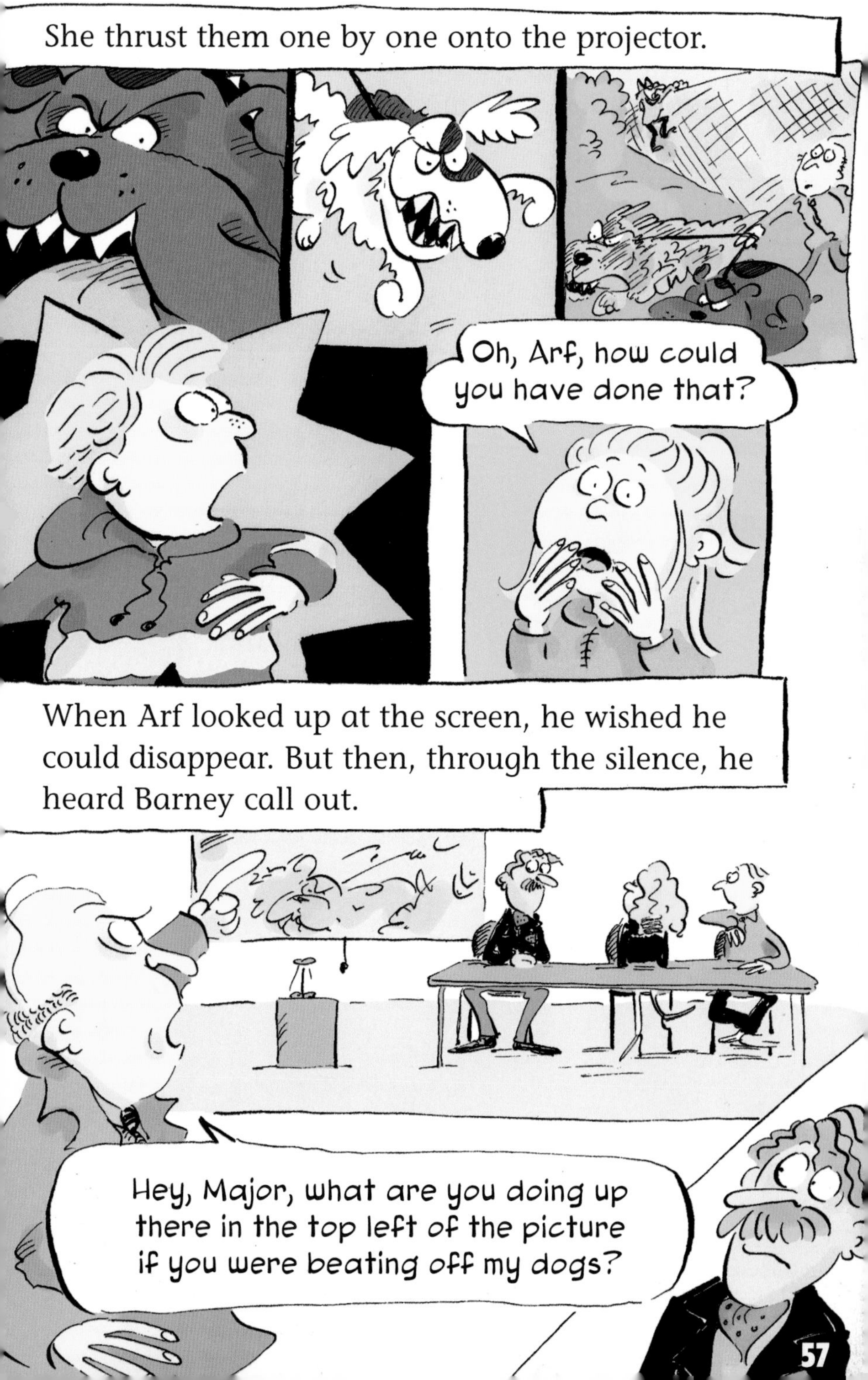
She thrust them one by one onto the projector.
Oh, Arf, how could you have done that?
When Arf looked up at the screen, he wished he could disappear. But then, through the silence, he heard Barney call out.
Hey, Major, what are you doing up there in the top left of the picture if you were beating off my dogs?

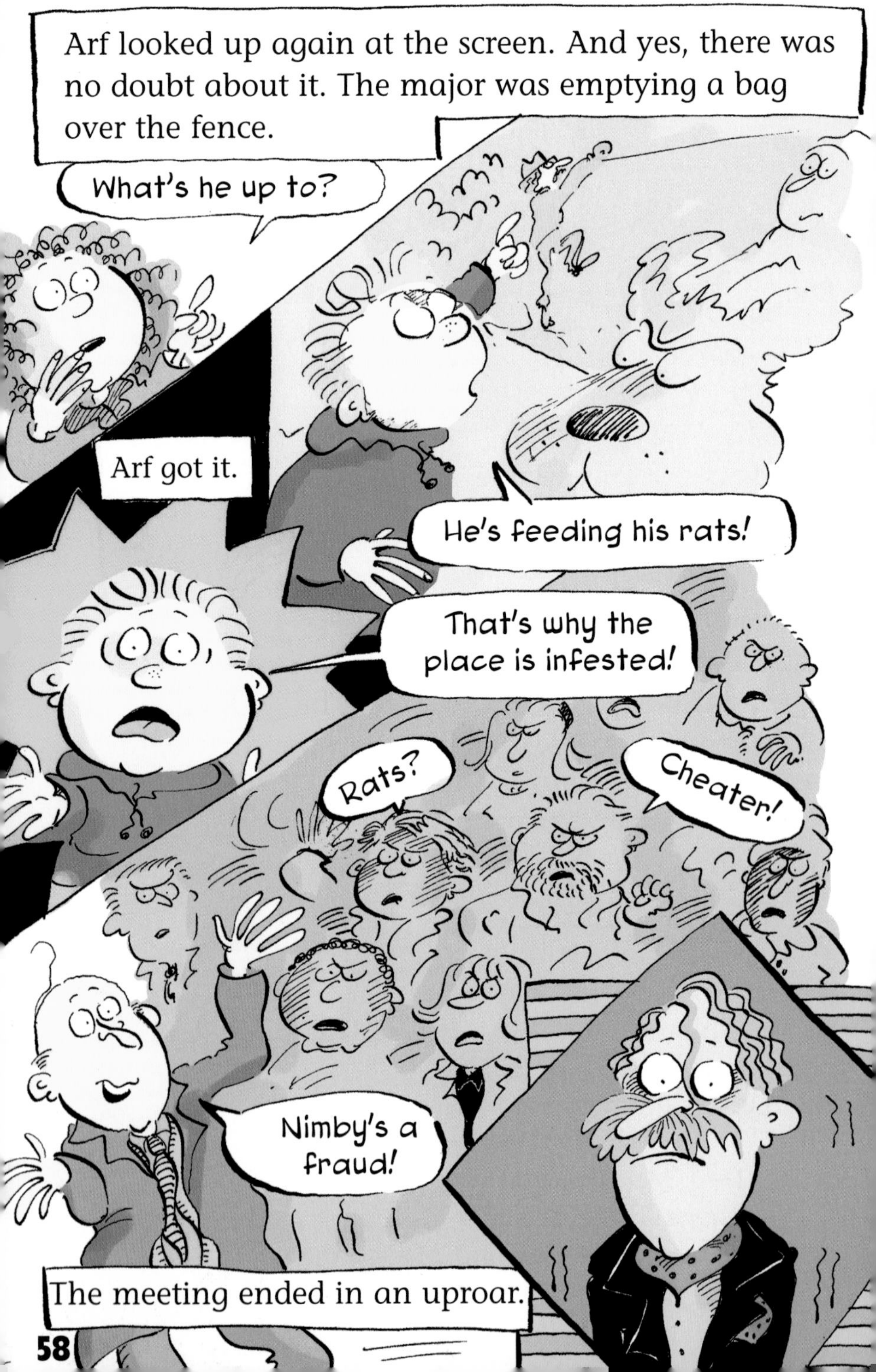
Arf looked up again at the screen. And yes, there was no doubt about it. The major was emptying a bag over the fence.
What's he up to?
Arf got it.
He's feeding his rats!
That's why the place is infested!
Rats?
Cheater!
Nimby's a fraud!
The meeting ended in an uproar.

CHAPTER SEVEN

Next Saturday, Arf went to the store to pick up the newspaper.

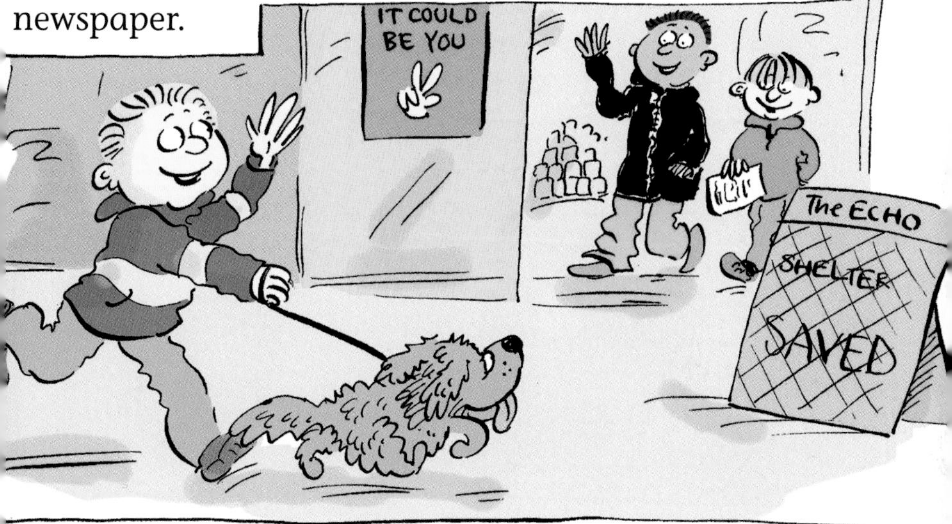
IT COULD BE YOU
The ECHO
SHELTER
SAVED

Back home, he opened the front door and was practically knocked off his feet by Barney's two big dogs with their big tongues, trying to lick his face, and . . .

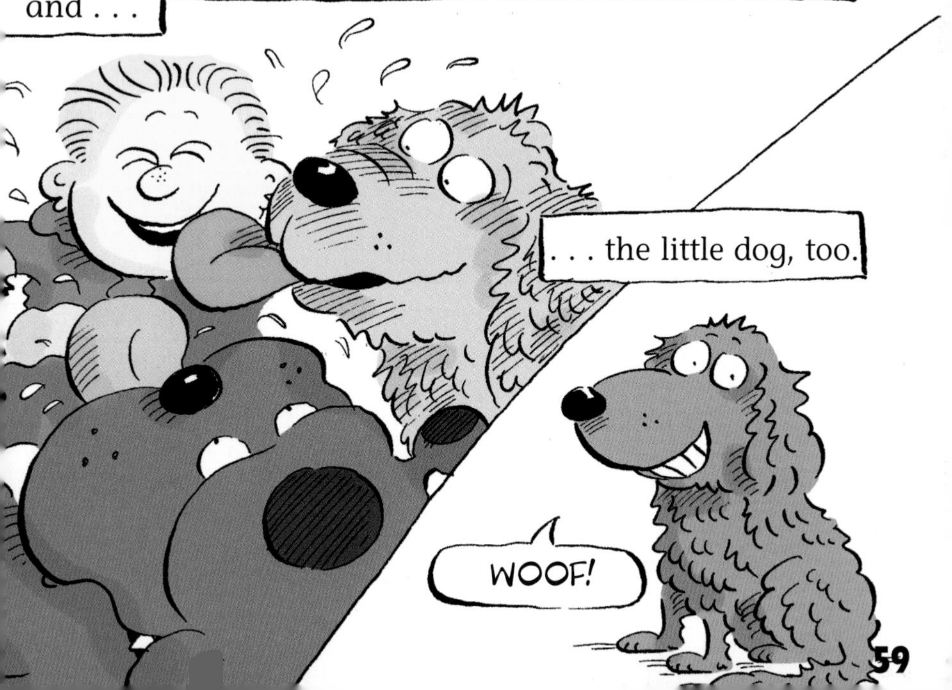
. . . the little dog, too.
WOOF!

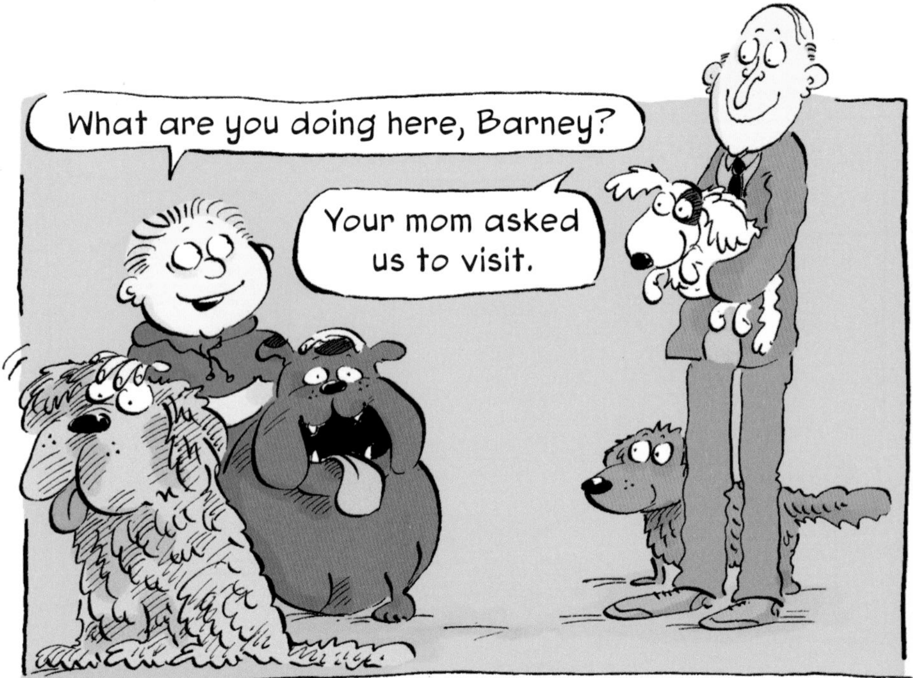
What are you doing here, Barney?
Your mom asked us to visit.

Behind him was Mr. Sanjay and Mrs. Hartlepool, who ran the animal shelter.

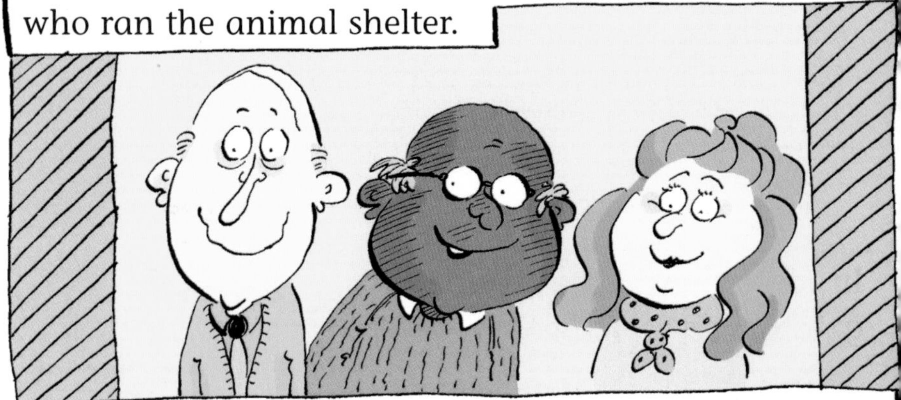

In the kitchen, there was a cake on the table and a present wrapped in striped paper.

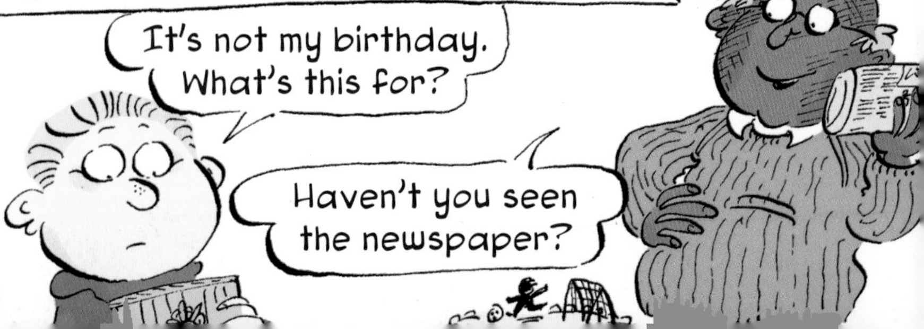
It's not my birthday. What's this for?
Haven't you seen the newspaper?

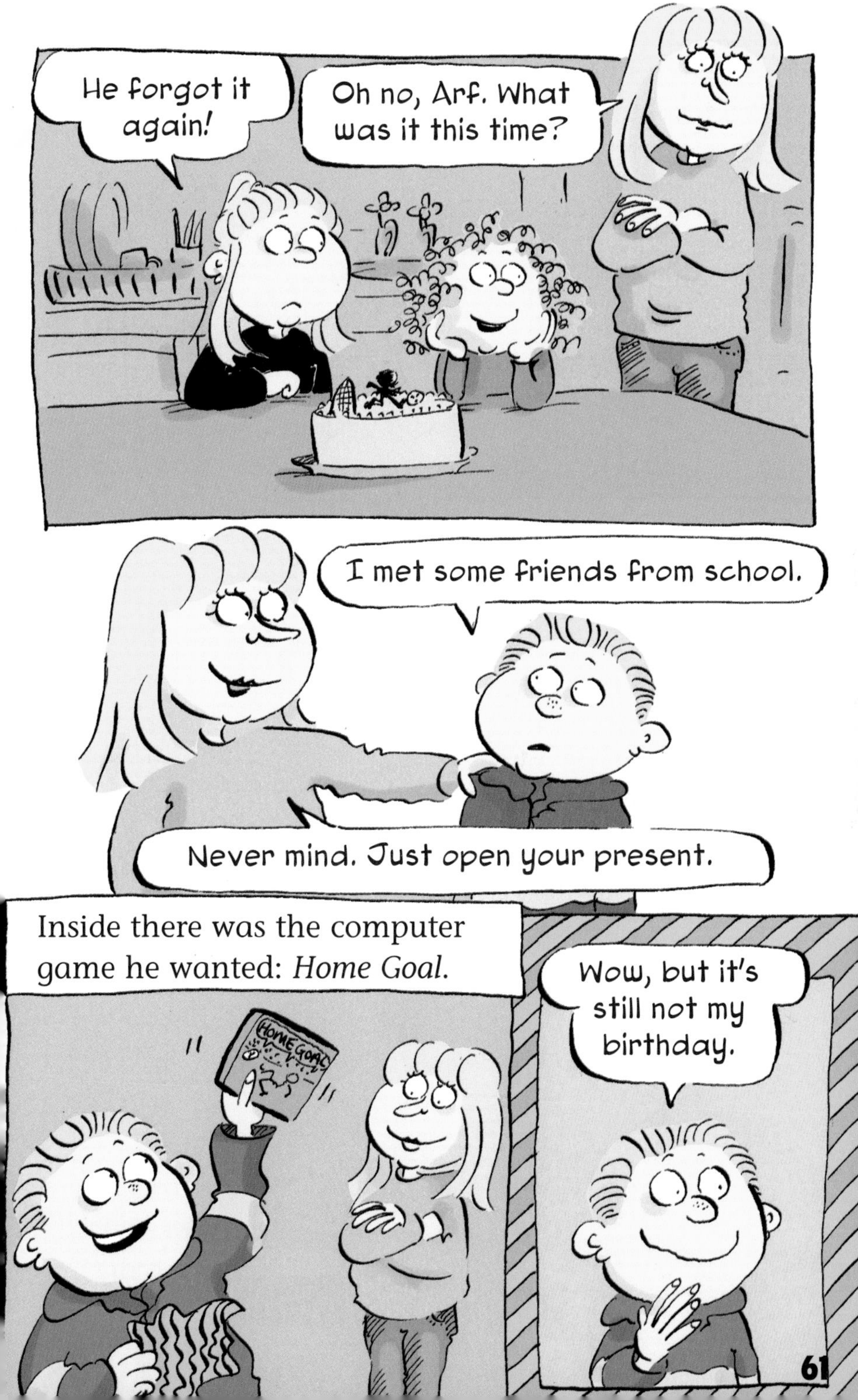
He forgot it again!
Oh no, Arf. What was it this time?
I met some friends from school.
Never mind. Just open your present.
Inside there was the computer game he wanted: *Home Goal*.
HOME GOAL
Wow, but it's still not my birthday.

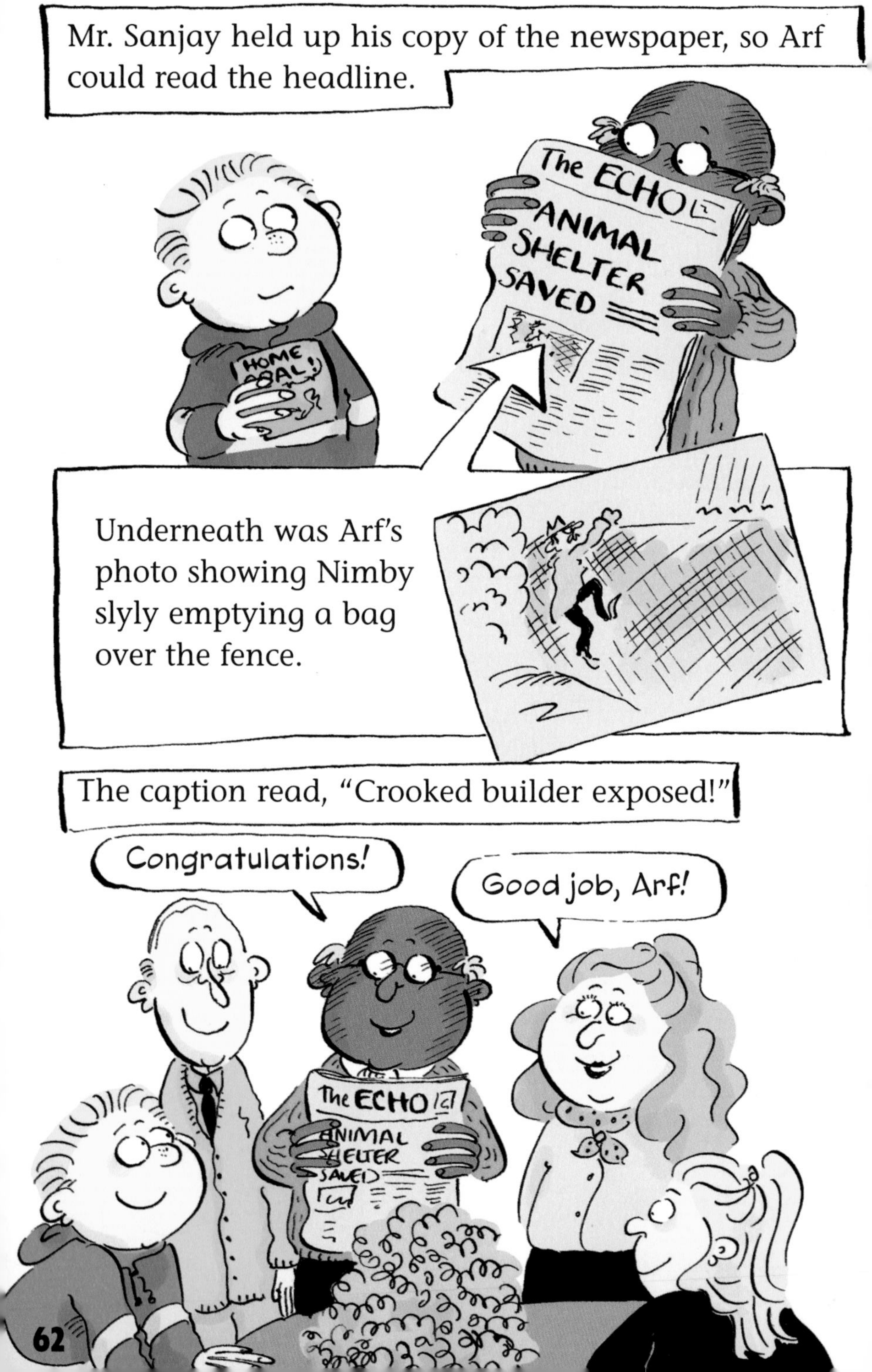
Mr. Sanjay held up his copy of the newspaper, so Arf could read the headline.
The ECHO
ANIMAL SHELTER SAVED
Underneath was Arf's photo showing Nimby slyly emptying a bag over the fence.
The caption read, "Crooked builder exposed!"
Congratulations!
Good job, Arf!
The ECHO
ANIMAL SHELTER SAVED

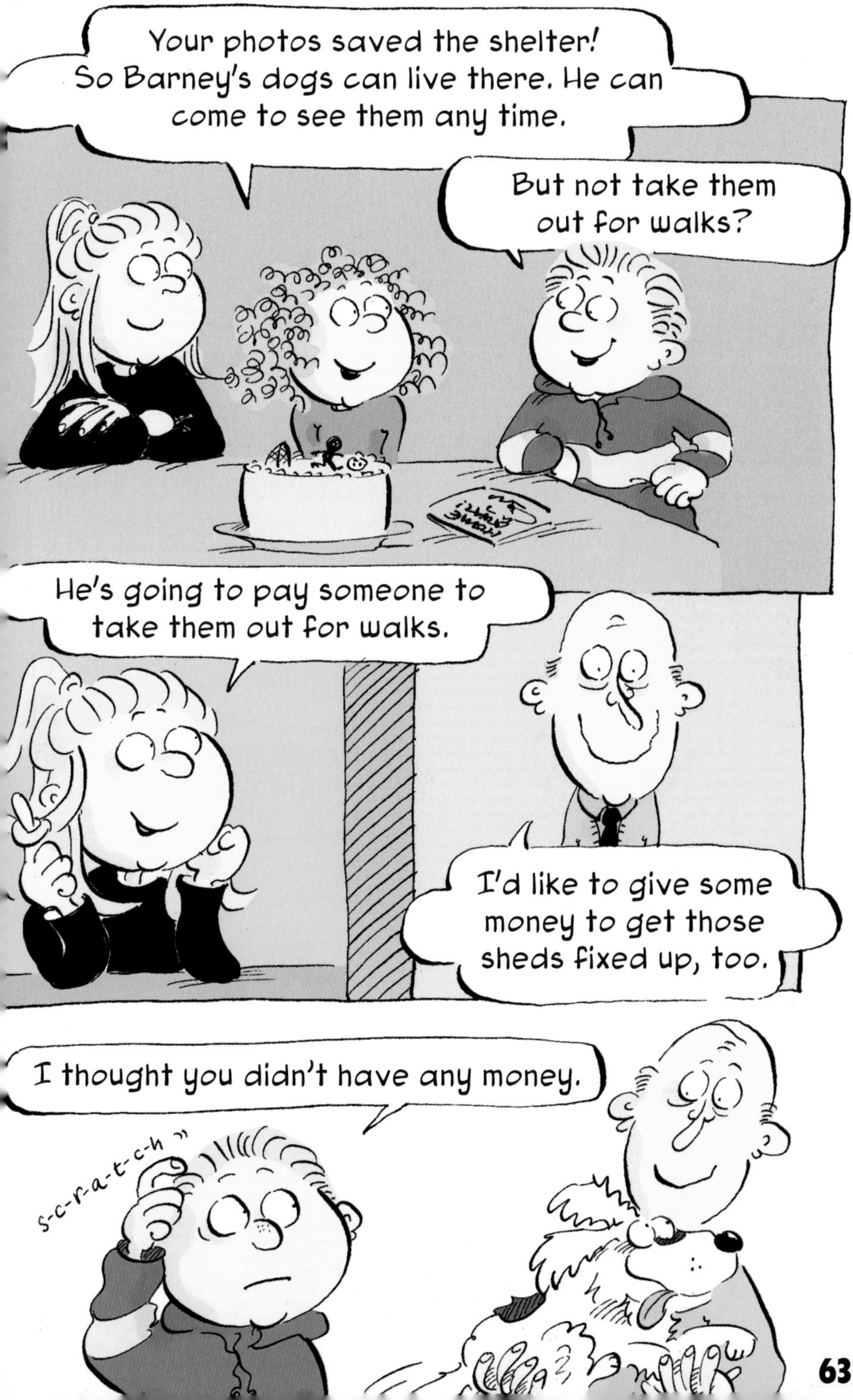
Your photos saved the shelter! So Barney's dogs can live there. He can come to see them any time.
But not take them out for walks?
He's going to pay someone to take them out for walks.
I'd like to give some money to get those sheds fixed up, too.
I thought you didn't have any money.
"s-c-r-a-t-c-h"

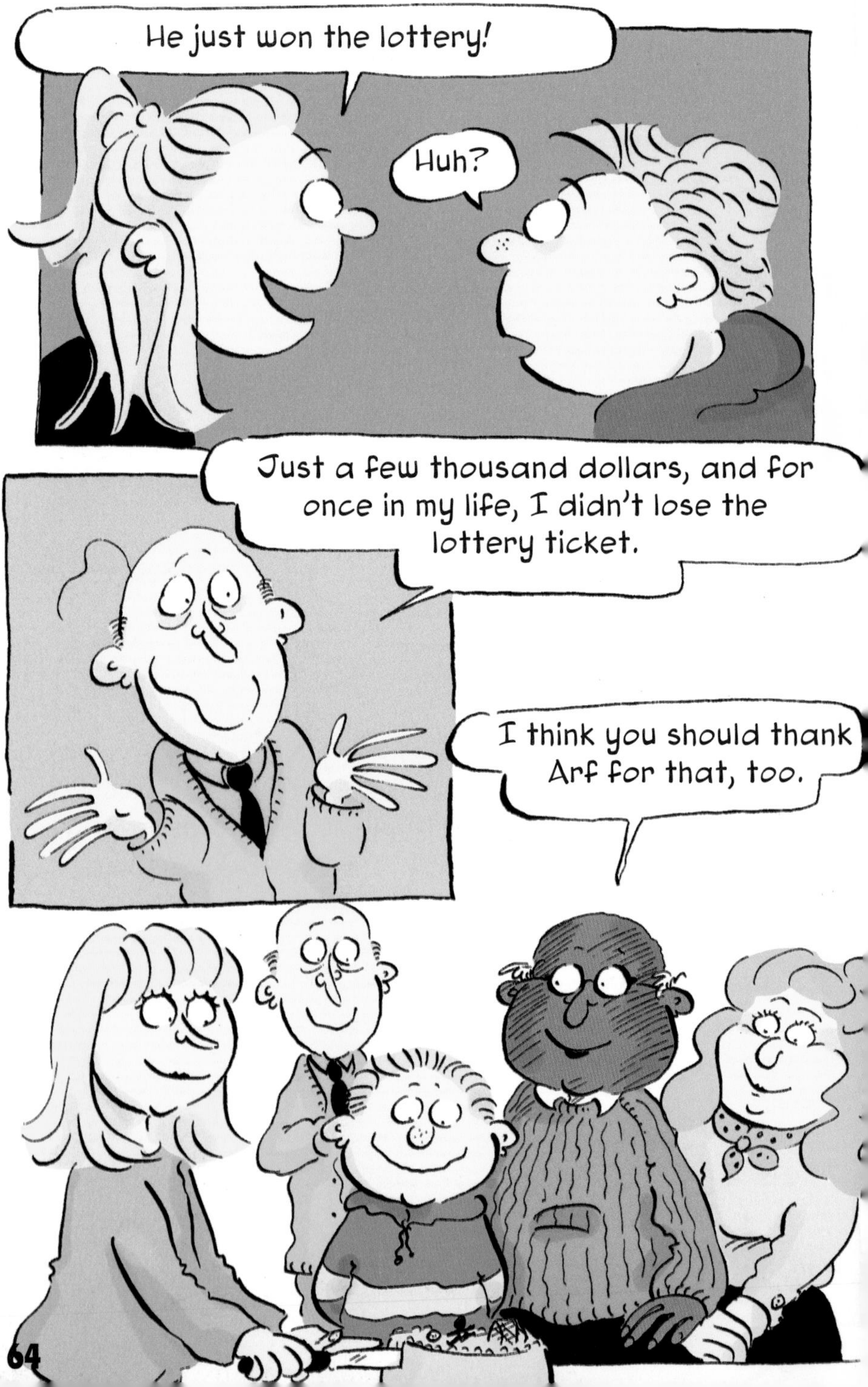
He just won the lottery!
Huh?
Just a few thousand dollars, and for once in my life, I didn't lose the lottery ticket.
I think you should thank Arf for that, too.

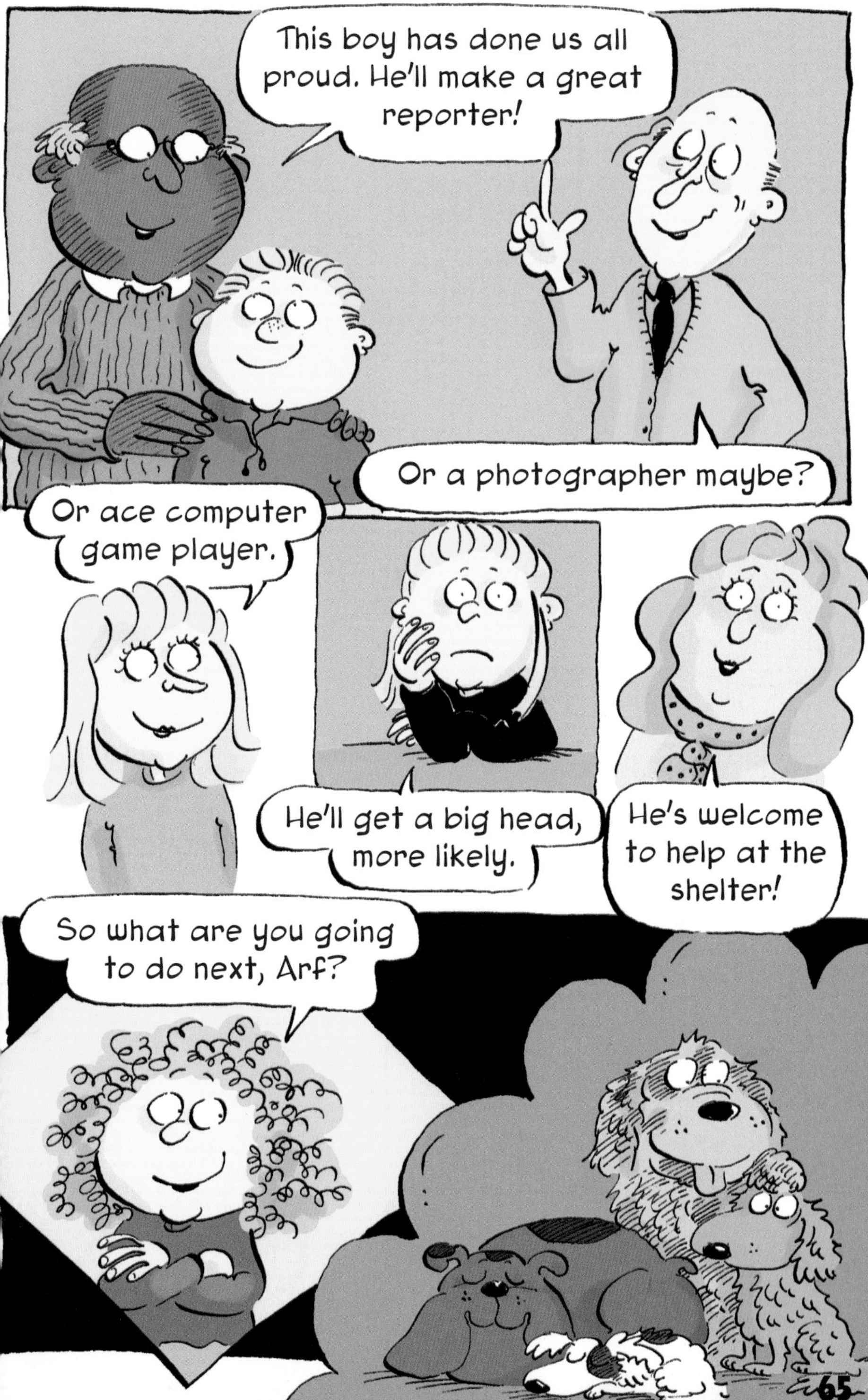
This boy has done us all proud. He'll make a great reporter!
Or a photographer maybe?
Or ace computer game player.
He'll get a big head, more likely.
He's welcome to help at the shelter!
So what are you going to do next, Arf?

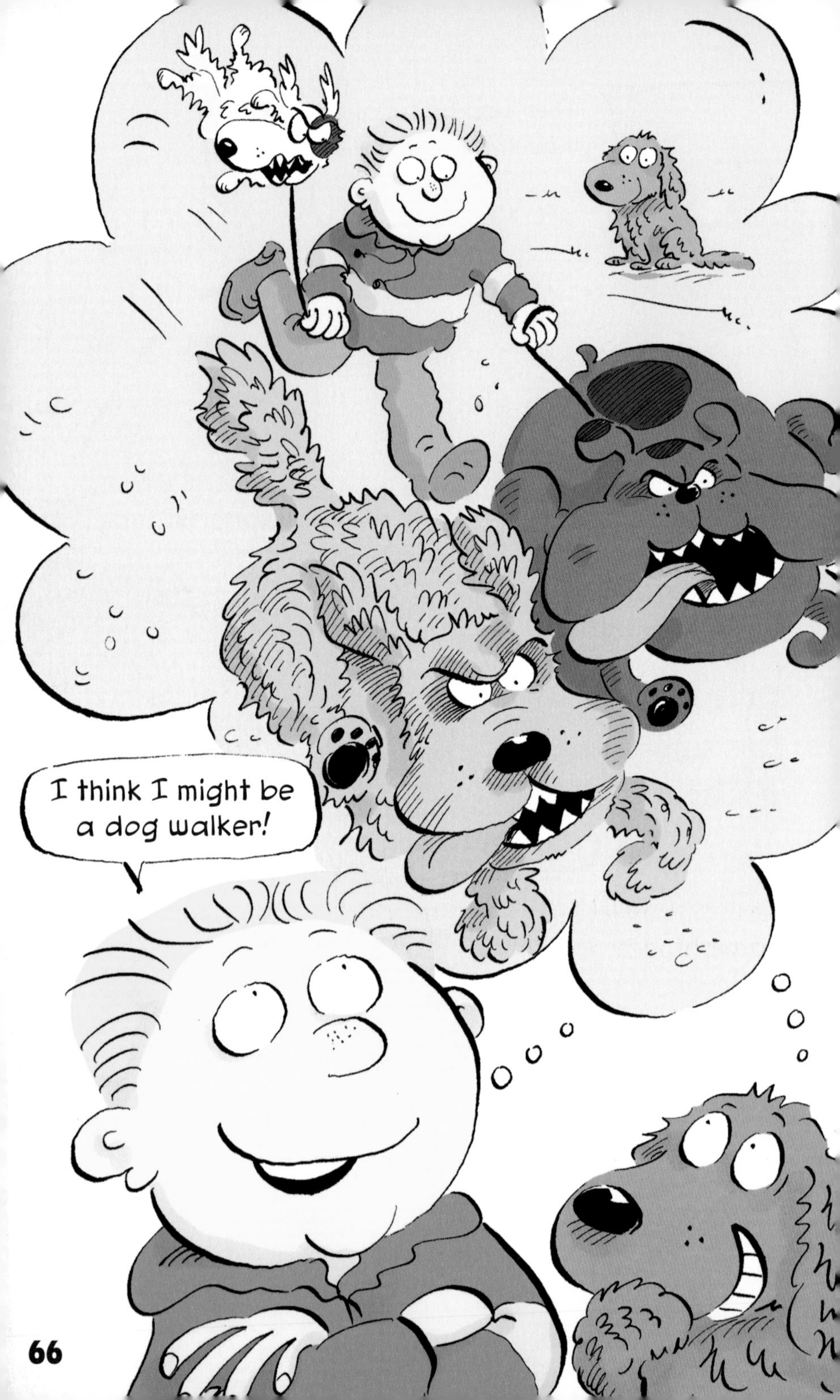
I think I might be a dog walker!

GLOSSARY

develop (di-VEL-uhp)—to treat camera film with chemicals in order to produce pictures

disease (duh-ZEEZ)—an illness

disturbance (di-STUR-buhnss)—something that bothers people

expose (ek-SPOZE)—to reveal the truth about someone or something

infested (in-FESS-tid)—full of unwanted things, such as animals or germs

innocent (IN-uh-suhnt)—not guilty

lottery (LOT-ur-ee)—a game people play for the chance to win a prize

menace (MEN-iss)—a threat to people

protest (PROH-test)—to state your beliefs against something in public

uproar (UP-ror)—noise and shouting

victim (VIK-tuhm)—a person who is tricked or treated unfairly

villain (VIL-uhn)—a bad or evil person

DISCUSSION QUESTIONS

1. Why does Arf believe Major Nimby's story about the rats?

2. Arf tries to take photographs to make money, but at the end of the story, he decides to walk dogs to earn money. Do you have chores that you do to make money? What are they?

3. Why does Major Nimby like Arf's photographs of the dogs?

WRITING PROMPTS

1. Sometimes the truth is difficult to see, such as when Arf believed the bad things Major Nimby told him about the animal shelter. Have you ever been fooled by someone who wasn't being honest? Write what that person told you. How did it make you feel?

2. Barney loves his three dogs. Describe your pet or a pet you wish you had.

3. There are two sides to every story. Imagine you are a newspaper reporter who saw a dog running loose in your neighborhood. First, write a story that makes people think the dog is causing problems. Second, write a story that makes people feel sorry for the dog.

ABOUT THE AUTHOR

Philip Wooderson has written more than twenty books for children, including the new young adult suspense novel, *The Plague, My Side of the Story*. Wooderson lives in England.

ABOUT THE ILLUSTRATOR

Bridget MacKeith says that being an illustrator is the only thing she has ever wanted to be. Although she once thought of being an opera singer! MacKeith's artwork appears in dozens of children's books.
She currently lives in a small town in the middle of the Salisbury Plain in England, with her husband, Gareth, her two children, and a big, hairy Newfoundland dog named Rudi. She also illustrates "a lot of cards for Hallmark."

ALSO BY PHILIP WOODERSON

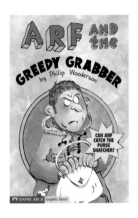

ARF AND THE
GREEDY GRABBER
by Philip Wooderson
CAN ARF CATCH THE PURSE SNATCHER?
STONE ARCH

Arf and the Greedy Grabber

Arf loves practical jokes. His tricks give him and his sisters a laugh . . . until a real thief turns up.

ARF AND THE
METAL DETECTOR
by Philip Wooderson
GRAPHIC NOVEL
STONE ARCH

Arf and the Metal Detector

Arf can't help himself. When a package for his neighbor shows up at his house, Arf has to see what's inside. The package leads him to more trouble, a couple of crooks, and a buried treasure.

ORDER NOW!

STONE ARCH BOOKS,
151 Good Counsel Hill Drive, Mankato, MN 56001
1-800-421-7731
www.stonearchbooks.com

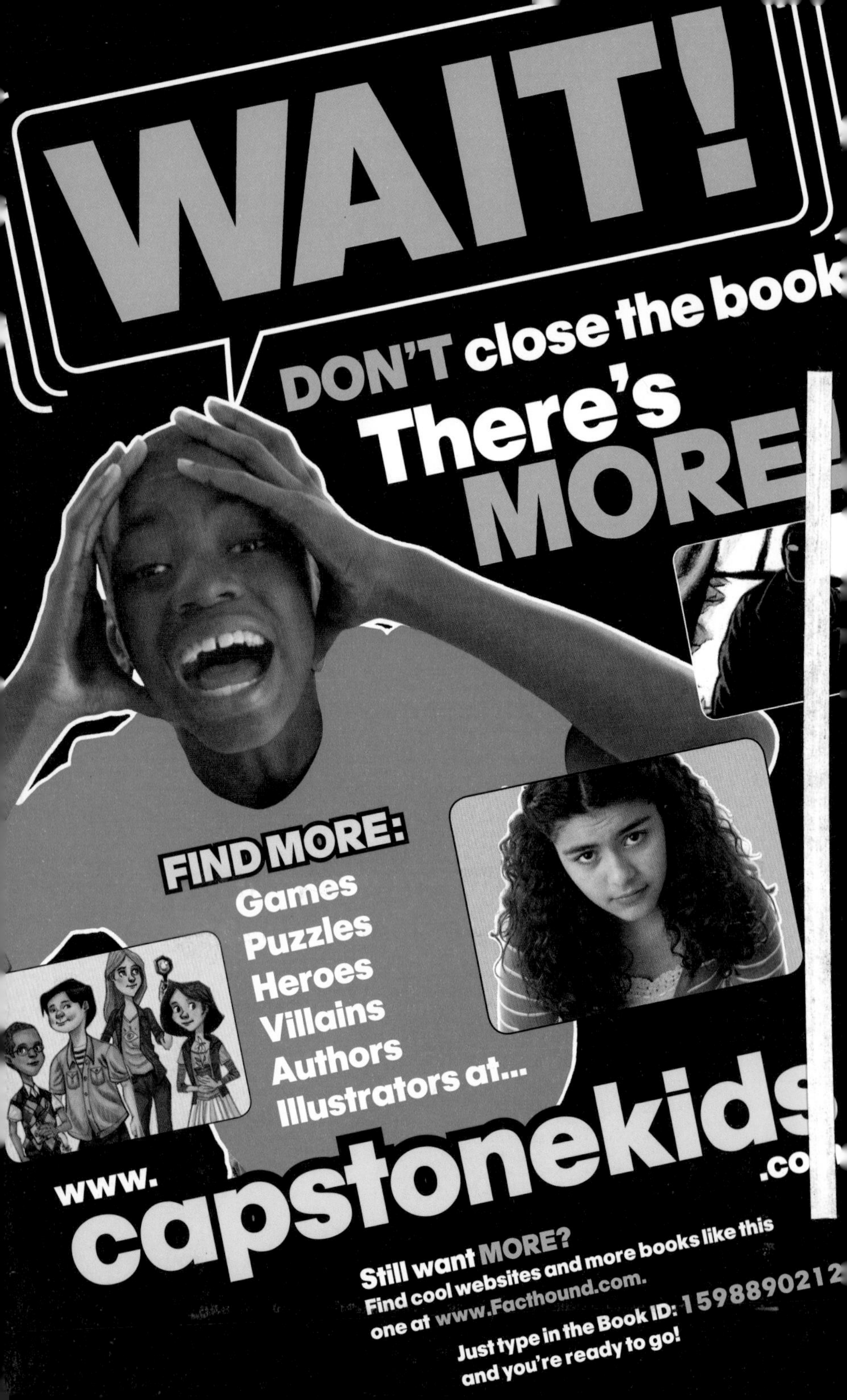

WAIT!
DON'T close the book
There's
MORE
FIND MORE:
Games
Puzzles
Heroes
Villains
Authors
Illustrators at...
www.
capstonekids
.co
Still want MORE?
Find cool websites and more books like this one at www.Facthound.com.
Just type in the Book ID: 1598890212
and you're ready to go!